He paused. He'd been about to say they shouldn't hurt each other. But that wasn't what he wanted to say. That said far too much. "Please, let's not push it . . ." he finally murmured.

Her eyes widened, and he could see she spoke from her heart. "Daniel, I don't even know what I'm pushing for."

He laughed then, softly, and drew his hand through the curling tendrils of her hair. That was an old gesture, left over from their past. Daniel could see by Cassandra's expression that she was remembering it, the same as he, and for some reason he wanted tonight to belong to the here and now.

"Let's go ride the roller coaster again," he said, drawing her back into the flow of tourists.

"So you've decided you like a thrill now and then, huh?"

He squeezed her hand. "I had forgotten how much fun thrills can be."

Cassandra knew he was talking about them, not a silly amusement park ride, and happiness spread through her. This time, when their car stopped just before the first slide, she kissed him. And as expected, her stomach was doing flip-flops before they even started over the edge. What a ride, she thought. What a crazy, glorious ride this might turn out to be.

Dear Reader:

Welcome to Silhouette! What better way to celebrate St. Valentine's Day and all the romance that goes with it than to indulge yourself with a Silhouette Desire?

If this is your first Desire, let me extend an invitation for you to sit back, kick off your shoes and enjoy. If you are a regular reader, you already know what awaits you.

A Silhouette Desire can encompass many varying moods and tones. The books can be deeply emotional and dramatic, or charming and lighthearted. But no matter what, each and every one is a sensual, compelling love story written by and for today's women.

I know you'll enjoy February's *Man of the Month*, *A Loving Spirit* by Annette Broadrick. But I think *all* of the February books are terrific. Give in to Desire . . . you'll be glad you did!

All the best,

Lucia Macro
Senior Editor

CELESTE HAMILTON

RUBY FIRE

SILHOUETTE *Desire*

Published by Silhouette Books New York

America's Publisher of Contemporary Romance

SILHOUETTE BOOKS
300 East 42nd St., New York, N.Y. 10017

ISBN: 0-373-05549-8

First Silhouette Books printing February 1990

All the characters in this book are fictitious. Any
resemblance to actual persons, living or dead, is
purely coincidental.

Books by Celeste Hamilton

Silhouette Special Edition

Torn Asunder #418
Silent Partner #447
A Fine Spring Rain #503
Face Value #532

Silhouette Desire

*The Diamond's Sparkle #537
*Ruby Fire #549

*Aunt Eugenia's Treasures trilogy

CELESTE HAMILTON

began writing when she was ten years old, with the encouragement of parents who told her she could do anything she set out to do and teachers who helped her refine her talents. The broadcast media captured her interest in high school, and she graduated from the University of Tennessee with a B.S. in Communications. From there she began writing and producing commercials at a Chattanooga, Tennessee, radio station.

Celeste began writing romances in 1985 and now works at her craft full-time. She says she "never intends to stop." Married to a policeman, she likes nothing better than spending time at home with him and their two much-loved cats, although she and her husband also enjoy traveling when their busy schedules permit. Wherever they go, however, "It's always nice to come home to East Tennessee—one of the most beautiful corners of the world."

For Vickie Hackney Bobitt

We've been friends
through all the twists of fate,
from D.O. to Bono,
from houses to husbands.
And just when I'm sure you're lost,
you pop back into my life.
I'm glad. Because you're always welcome.
No retreat, no surrender, right, Vic?

One

The office building was glass and steel, a towering window-washer's bonanza. By night it probably glowed with lights from within. But on this sunny June morning, it was a tall many-sided mirror. Like stained glass, the upper-story windows captured the colors of the cloud-dotted horizon and the Nashville skyline, while the windows below reflected a flower-filled courtyard.

Beside one of those ground-floor windows, Cassandra Martin paused to study her wavy reflection. "I don't look desperate enough, do I?" she said to the woman standing at her side.

Eugenia Davis's blue-eyed gaze, undimmed by eighty years of living, swept Cassandra from head to toe. "Well, red might not have been the absolute best choice for groveling."

"I guess I'm not used to groveling."

"Come now, dear, I've seen you wheedle thousands out of your father."

Cassandra made a face. "Wheedling and groveling aren't the same thing. And besides, this isn't Daddy we're going to see. It would be easy if it were. With Daddy, I can always get into character for getting money. I even know the right costume to wear—silk and pearls."

"Perhaps you should have drawn on your theatrical training to come up with the right costume for soliciting charitable donations."

"I did, but this is the most conservative outfit I own," Cassandra retorted, though both she and Eugenia knew it was a lie. In Cassandra's flamboyant but extensive wardrobe, she could have found something tamer than her short red skirt and matching jacket. But she had decided early this morning it was a little-red-suit sort of day, no matter who she had to see. The sky was deep blue, and the air had been washed clean by last night's rain. Even here in the city, the world sparkled.

June in the South. Nothing else compared, Cassandra decided, though she'd spent summers in Brazil, London, New York and Australia. Even when the temperature soared and the humidity settled on Nashville like dampened wool, she loved being here. It had taken her too long to realize she belonged right where she'd begun.

Filling her lungs with a deep breath of air, she tossed her head, and the dark hair she had subdued into a chignon tumbled over her shoulders. "Oh, blast." She raked an impatient hand through the curls. The image of herself mirrored in the window lost even a hint of conservatism. She sighed. "Let's face it, Eugenia,

I'm just not the groveling type—even when it's for a good cause. Maybe we should forget about this.''

"Now, now, we'll have none of that kind of talk." Taking Cassandra's elbow in a grip surprisingly strong for a woman her age, Eugenia headed for the entrance. "I have it on good authority that Mr. Black is leaving town tomorrow and going on a very long trip. You have to see him today if you expect to obtain some financing for the school."

"But he doesn't even know we're coming."

"I thought we agreed that a surprise attack was the best way to handle this."

"*We* didn't agree on anything. This was your idea, remember?" Cassandra pointed out as she pulled the glass entry doors open. "I was all for calling the man up and inviting him to lunch."

"How very mundane. Not your style at all, my dear."

"Well, I've been brushing up on my mundane since I started trying to get funding for this school. A flick of the eyelashes doesn't always work with bureaucrats."

"That's no reason to become predictable." With her chin held at its usual regal tilt, Eugenia swept across the lobby, trailed by the scent of Chanel. Two businessmen halted their discussion to watch the progress of her trim lilac-clad figure.

Cassandra had to smile. She hoped to have Eugenia's pizzazz fifty years from now. Glancing back at the businessmen, Cassandra's smile deepened as she realized their admiring attention had shifted to herself. Not bad, she decided. The one in the owlish glasses was attractive in a scholarly sort of way.

"Are you coming, dear?" Eyebrows arched slightly, Eugenia turned from the opening elevator doors. Cassandra spared a regretful smile for her admirers as she followed her inside.

"I believe your attention-getting ensemble was the best choice after all," Eugenia said dryly as she pushed a button for the top floor. "Herb...I mean Mr. Black...is fond of pretty women."

Cassandra slanted her a sideways glance. "You certainly seem to know a lot about this Mr. Black. Is he your new beau?"

"I know him." Eugenia's tone was evasive, and she dismissed the question with a toss of her head. "But all you need be concerned with is that he is a true philanthropist, especially when it comes to young people who need help. He made his fortune the hard way, and I'm positive he's the perfect person to provide the extra funds you need for the school."

"You know," Cassandra mused, frowning. "Although I said I didn't know Mr. Black, I think I have heard of him."

"Of course you have," Eugenia replied so quickly that Cassandra glanced at her in surprise. The older woman rushed on. "Perhaps your parents have mentioned him. He's always in the papers—"

"You know Mother and Daddy aren't speaking to me right now, and I haven't had time to read the papers in weeks." Frowning, Cassandra watched the lights flash from numeral to numeral as the elevator climbed to the top of the building. "I'm just sure I've heard someone else discussing Mr. Black. Fairly recently, too. I wonder where?"

The elevator glided to a halt, and with another dismissive toss of her expertly coiffed white hair, Eugenia started down the hall. "The only thing you need concentrate on now is shaking a coupla hundred thou loose from Black's money tree."

Cassandra grinned at Eugenia's authentic-sounding tough talk. Given the unconventional twists and turns of the woman's life, it was entirely possible she had shaken other money trees. For Eugenia had a taste for adventure. That was just one of the reasons Cassandra adored her.

Cassandra had been ten years old the summer Eugenia had come home to Nashville. Arriving with trunks brimming with a lifetime of treasures, and accompanied by Jeannette, her French cook and housekeeper, Eugenia had moved in with her niece's family. The family included Cassandra's best friend, Liz Patterson. Liz and Eugenia had formed an instant bond, despite the half century separating them in age. That bond had soon widened to include Liz's friends, Maggie O'Grady and Cassandra.

Cassandra knew she and Liz and Maggie were the children Eugenia had never had. She felt closer to this woman than she'd ever felt to any blood relative. They were kindred spirits. Cassandra could remember looking into Eugenia's eyes and knowing instantly that here was someone who shared her restless yearning to know what lay beyond the next bend of the river.

Like Eugenia before her, Cassandra had left home at eighteen, despite the protests of parents who, while often indulgent, neither understood nor approved of their daughter's choices. Eugenia had set out to become a photojournalist. Her career had been less than spectacular, but her life had been full of adventure. In much the same way, Cassandra had bounced from acting to singing and dancing and now to teaching.

With every bounce, she had found the excitement she craved.

And Eugenia always supported me, Cassandra thought, sending the woman a fond glance. *Now that I'm ready to settle down, she's the only one who believes I've truly found my life's work.* As the two of them paused at the end of the foyer, Cassandra linked her arm through Eugenia's. "Thanks for your help," she whispered.

Eugenia patted her hand. "I just want you to have what you need, dear."

Cassandra got the fleeting impression that Eugenia was referring to something more than financing for the school. Suspicion nibbled at the back of her brain while she studied the discreet brass nameplate that read Herbert P. Black Enterprises, Inc. Where had she heard that name? Not knowing was maddening. But there wasn't time to ask the question again before Eugenia pushed open the door and sailed across a thick Aubusson carpet. *She's rather like an avalanche,* Cassandra thought. *Unstoppable.* Behind the teakwood desk, a young receptionist let her eyes widen as Eugenia drew to a halt.

"Mr. Black, please," Eugenia requested in a clear, firm voice, giving her name.

"I'm sorry, he's in a meeting. If you'd care—"

"Call him out."

Feeling uneasy, Cassandra fiddled with the strap of her oversized purse. Gutsy flamboyance was fine. She had employed it herself on many occasions, but it seemed as if Eugenia were going too far today. Mr. Herbert P. Black was going to throw them out on their ears.

"Call him," Eugenia said, a trifle more insistently.

The receptionist sputtered. Cassandra could have sworn she swallowed her gum. "I'm sorry—"

"This is an emergency." Eugenia placed her hands on the edge of the desk and leaned forward. The amethysts in her earrings flashed. *"Call him,"* she repeated, her eyes as friendly as those of a snake about to strike.

Apparently convinced she couldn't handle Eugenia on her own, the receptionist fled the room via the frosted glass door behind her desk.

"Emergency?" Cassandra murmured.

Eugenia patted her hand. "Just play it as we planned."

"But—"

Her protest was cut short by the arrival of a thunderstorm. For surely the man who rumbled through the door was Thor, the Norse god of thunder. He was tall and straight and hard of feature, with curling hair that gleamed white against his ruddy skin. Even his voice was booming. "Miss Eugenia Davis, what in the world—"

Eugenia shoved Cassandra forward. "This young woman has a problem."

For a moment Cassandra faltered. Then she caught the sparkle in the man's silvery eyes. *The old faker.* She hazarded a quick glance at Eugenia and saw the hastily concealed twitch of the woman's lips. What kind of plot were these two hatching?

"Well," Mr. Black bellowed. "Are you going to tell me about this emergency of yours, young lady?"

"Yes, go ahead," Eugenia prompted.

Thoroughly confused, Cassandra glanced from one to the other again. Heaven only knows what these senior citizen pranksters had up their sleeves, but if it was melodrama they were after, she could provide it as well as they. Casting her eyes demurely downward, she began in a trembling whisper, "My problem is my school, Mr. Black. Unless I find someone to help me, I'll have to close it, and all those kids..." She continued in the same low, sweet voice, explaining her school and its need.

Applause came from behind Mr. Black, catching Cassandra off guard. More confused than ever, she looked toward the door and into a pair of brown eyes as familiar as her own.

Daniel O'Grady's eyes.

"Congratulations, Miss Martin," he said in a voice she could have recognized among hundreds, even if it was as cold and disapproving as it had once been warm and happy.

"Daniel," she whispered. "Where—"

"No, please do continue," he insisted, propping one well-pressed gray-flannel shoulder against the doorjamb. She could remember when he had worn sloppy clothes and an even sloppier haircut. Now the unruly light brown curls had been cut away. She much preferred his hair the old way, just as she preferred the boy Daniel had been to the man he was now.

"Give us a show, Cass," he continued, slipping into the nickname only he had ever used. "It's not everyone who can so eloquently reprise 'The Little Match Girl' character they created in the fourth grade."

So that's what I was drawing on. She stared at him, surprised that he could recognize what had been purely unconscious on her part.

"So you know my right-hand man, do you?" Mr. Black said, perching on the edge of the desk where the astounded-looking receptionist had slipped back into her chair.

Cassandra swallowed. "Daniel is your...man?" she whispered, looking at Mr. Black.

"I told you who I worked for," Daniel said, an accusation in his voice.

Told her? Cassandra started to shake her head. Then she remembered the last time she'd seen Daniel—at Liz's wedding three months ago. He'd been sipping champagne, standing beside the parlor doors at Liz's parents' home. In his black tuxedo, he had looked tall and straight and handsome—heartbreakingly so. Though, like her, he had been part of the wedding party, she had managed to avoid him until they had accidentally found themselves standing together at the reception.

If Cassandra recalled correctly, they had made stiff, inane small talk, the same kind of conversations they'd been having for the twelve years since he had refused to forgive her. Perhaps that was where she had heard Mr. Black's name, but it was no wonder she had almost blocked it out. The only thing she remembered clearly about that conversation was wishing Daniel would look *at* her, not *through* her. She had hoped on that day of all days, at the wedding of someone they both loved, that he would finally smile at her again. Twelve years was a long time to do without Daniel's smile.

Now his lips curved into the cardboardlike grin he used whenever she was around. God, how she hated that.

"Cassandra and I knew each other," he was saying to Mr. Black. "Once upon a time."

Fairy-tale beginnings, Cassandra thought. *It's a pity the happily-ever-after didn't come so easily.*

Daniel looked back at her. "Cassandra is quite an actress, Mr. Black."

"So I've hea—" A sharp glance from Eugenia had the man ending his words on a cough. Cassandra's eyes narrowed, her suspicions becoming concrete. This was all a setup. "I assumed she was an actress," Mr. Black corrected, trying to regain the same blustering pose he'd held only moments before. "That's why she has this school, right, Eugen...uh...Miss Davis?"

"Come now, Cassandra," Daniel prompted before Eugenia could reply. "Weren't you going to ask Mr. Black for something? Don't let me interrupt your dramatic entreaty."

Flushing with anger at his sarcasm, Cassandra glared instead at Eugenia. This was all her doing. Now that Liz was happily settled with Nathan, Eugenia wouldn't rest until Cassandra and Maggie were married off, too. She'd been in a matchmaking frenzy for months, and she had always thought Daniel and Cassandra should get back together.

Damn her for her tricks, Cassandra thought. Her glance wandered back to Daniel. Even with his lips twisted so scornfully, he was appealing. He had always been appealing. Her mouth went dry. Damn, she repeated silently.

Damn Eugenia for knowing me so well.

"Dear—" the older woman began.

Cassandra cut her short by turning to Mr. Black. "As I was saying, sir—" she flicked a glance at Daniel "—before we were so rudely interrupted..." If Daniel thought she had been dramatic before, she'd give him drama now. She drew a deep breath and slipped into a breathless, Deep South-flavored dialect. "Sir, you are a stranger, but if you would be so kind—"

"Blanche DuBois, from *Streetcar*," Daniel interrupted. "Your junior year in high school."

Ignoring him, Cassandra stood with arms akimbo and lifted her chin in belligerent challenge. "Aye, guv'nor—"

"Eliza Doolittle," Daniel cut in. "*My Fair Lady*, sophomore year."

He thinks he's so smart. I'll show him something he never saw me do. Though she was really playing to Daniel, Cassandra kept her attention focused on an appreciative Mr. Black. She slipped a hand through her hair, letting the long, curling tendrils drift slowly to her shoulder. Her other hand slid over the curve of her hip. She moistened her lips.

"Maggie, the cat," Daniel whispered before she could speak.

Surprised, Cassandra jerked her gaze to his again. "How did you know? You never saw—"

"*Cat on a Hot Tin Roof*, off-off-Broadway, six years ago," he continued. "Your best roles were always Tennessee Williams." Color flooded his cheeks then, and his mouth thinned into an annoyed line.

Cassandra forgot herself enough to let the excited bubbles dancing in her stomach show in her voice. "You saw that production?"

"Yeah, I did." Daniel straightened from the doorway, silently cursing himself. What a fool he was to tell her that. He cleared his throat, studiously avoiding Cassandra's sparkling ebony eyes. He looked instead at his boss. "Since it's obvious that Miss Martin has a presentation to make, wouldn't we all be much more comfortable in the conference room?''

"I was rather enjoying the show right here," Mr. Black replied, smiling at Cassandra. "Though I think I want to hear a little more about this school of yours before I write you a check."

"A check?" Cassandra echoed, sounding surprised.

"Sir," Daniel began disapprovingly.

Eugenia slipped her arm through his, forcing him to turn from Cassandra. "Dan, my boy, it's been far too long since you've come for dinner, and I've been wanting to talk to you about this horrid man your sister is dating."

With a sigh of resignation, Daniel let himself be swept away by Eugenia's chatter as they headed toward the conference room. She was one of the few people he allowed to totally distract him. He was fond of her, used to her affected eccentricities and the way she tried to direct the lives of those she loved. He owed Eugenia Davis for many kindnesses, and Daniel O'Grady never forgot a debt. When he and Maggie had needed help after their mother died, Eugenia had stepped in. Quietly. Without fuss. The same way she had introduced him to Herbert Black years ago. But an introduction had been all he needed. Daniel knew he had earned his "right-hand man" status on his own.

And because he took his job seriously, he had to be concerned about his boss writing Cassandra a check for any amount of money. The man had plenty of money to spare, and he had purchased entire companies on a whim. Daniel, however, couldn't sit still while money was wasted on one of Cassandra's harebrained schemes. There were at least a thousand other good uses to which the funds could be put.

Maggie had kept him posted on this latest installment in the continuing saga of Cassandra's madcap life. He knew Cassandra had invested a hefty portion of her own money in the school, but he had tried not to listen to details. The knowledge that Cassandra was back in Nashville was disturbing enough. He hadn't needed the extra burden of thinking she might actually stay.

Burden? Why was it he still couldn't dismiss Cassandra the way she had once dismissed him? Gritting his teeth in frustration, he pulled out a chair for Eugenia.

She patted his cheek in exactly the same manner she had used when he was twelve. "Now, Daniel, you know you're much more attractive when you smile."

He had to laugh as he took the chair beside hers, but the laughter died when he turned to find Cassandra in the doorway. Her scarlet-tinted lips pouted a little, but fire flashed from her eyes. Shoulders straight, she swept to the table in her best Eugenia-ish style. She sat down opposite him, a challenge evident in every line of her body, every lush feminine curve of all five-foot-two of her. . . .

Realizing that he was dwelling on exactly what he should avoid, Daniel cleared his throat, prepared to explain to Mr. Black just how flighty and irresponsible Cassandra was.

But Mr. Black forestalled him with a wave of his hand. "Let's hear from Miss Martin."

Cassandra obliged, without the dramatics. Daniel had to admit her school was a great idea. This spring, they had begun offering free-of-charge after-school and weekend programs in drama and music to children from economically disadvantaged families. Her intent was to supplement the programs offered by the public school system. On staff, she had another drama teacher, several part-time music and dance instructors and a full-time counselor.

"Why a counselor?" Daniel asked.

"Because some of these kids have some real problems," Cassandra replied. "In many cases, taking our classes provides an outlet for their feelings and their undirected energies and frustrations. Along with developing their talents, I want the school to be a place where they know they'll be listened to."

"Sounds as if you're biting off more than you can chew," Daniel muttered. "As usual," he added softly.

Cassandra glared at him. "I'll have you know that for three months we've done just fine. And this summer, we're booked solid with participants. The high-school kids are putting on three plays. We've got fifth graders who are writing musicals, for heaven's sake. We're keeping these kids busy and involved and out of trouble."

"It really is marvelous," Eugenia put in.

"And very ambitious," Daniel added with eyebrows raised. "How long are you planning to stay with it, Cassandra?"

He was provoking her, but Cassandra didn't take the bait. Instead, she appealed to Mr. Black. "I have the funds to see us through the rest of the summer and the first part of the fall school semester, but beyond that I need additional backing." From her briefcase-sized purse, she withdrew a folder. Without so much as a glance at the contents, Mr. Black passed it to Daniel. That made Cassandra frown. But in a cool, professional manner that surprised him, she gave the names of her prestigious-sounding board of directors. "Every one of them will be willing to vouch for my dedication to this project," she finished with a triumphant look at Daniel.

"Of course," he said, glancing up from the unexpectedly neat financial statement. "They're all friends of your family, aren't they? They probably wouldn't say anything bad about Claire and William's little girl."

"That's not fair," she protested.

"Really?" Daniel shut the folder. "If these people have so much faith in you, why aren't they bankrolling this scheme?"

"This isn't a *scheme*," Cassandra denied, finally letting her temper get away from her. "And many of them have already made hefty contributions, as you'll see if you take the time to look through those papers before you dismiss me."

Mr. Black broke through the brewing storm. "I think you've got something good going, Miss Martin, and I'd like to contribute to the cause." He smiled at Daniel's scowl.

"I'd prefer it if I had a chance to go over these statements," Daniel protested. "I know Cassandra, and—"

"Don't you mean you *knew* her," Eugenia cut in.

"Yes," Mr. Black agreed, grinning. "I believe you said earlier that you had known her *once upon a time*."

"But she's still—"

"As charming as she ever was, I'm sure," Mr. Black finished for him. Daniel was left groping for a comeback while his boss got to his feet. "In fact,

Daniel, since you and Miss Martin are acquainted, why don't you just oversee this entire endowment? I'm thinking of a sum of about . . ." He paused for a moment and then named an amount twice what Cassandra had hoped for. Mr. Black continued, "With an investment of that scope, I'll expect you to work very closely with Miss Martin. I know you'll see that the money is put to good use."

Just what I want, Cassandra thought, to work closely with a resentful, disapproving Daniel. She could see he was no happier about the arrangement. Angry color was staining his cheeks again, but he said nothing.

Mr. Black looked at his watch. "Tell you what, Daniel. Why don't you go on over to the school with Miss Martin right now? You can give me a report. I know you'll tell me if I'm wasting my money."

"I'm sorry," Daniel replied. "But my afternoon isn't free."

"You could clear it."

Though Mr. Black's tone was mild, Daniel recognized a direct order. There'd been few of those in the years he had worked for this man, so arguing with him over such a small request seemed petty. With a sidelong glance at Eugenia, Daniel wondered just what sort of strings the woman was pulling. She merely widened her eyes and sat with her hands folded on the table, the picture of innocence.

"Care to join us?" Daniel asked her. "It's obvious how very interested you are in Cassandra's school."

"No, you young people run along without me." With calculated grace, Eugenia touched her hair. "I'm sure Mr. Black could be persuaded to see me home. That wouldn't be too much trouble, would it?"

"The honor will be mine," Mr. Black replied with a tiny bow in her direction.

Cassandra smothered a smile. The blustering Thor had been reduced to a lovesick suitor. Lord help the man. She glanced at Daniel's frown and decided divine intervention might also be of some help to her this afternoon. She gathered her courage, stood and held out her hand to Mr. Black. "Thank you for your help."

"My pleasure." There were again sparkles in the depths of his gray eyes. "You're a very persuasive young woman."

She nodded in Eugenia's direction. "Oh, I think I had a great deal of help in the persuasion department. Before I even got here." Everyone shared a good-natured chuckle.

Everyone, that is, but Daniel.

"Let's get this over with," he suggested in the most impatient of tones.

Laughing, Cassandra fluttered her eyelashes at him. "My, but the women must jump when you act so masterful, Mr. O'Grady."

He muttered something unintelligible, and she laughed again. She wasn't going to let Daniel get her down. In fact, she was going to prove to him how wrong he was. She had come a long way from the flighty, irresponsible girl she'd once been. With a last wave to Eugenia and Mr. Black, she followed Daniel out of the conference room.

When the door had closed behind them, Mr. Black sat down and crossed his arms. "Poor Daniel. She's going to keep him jumping."

Eugenia stiffened. "Daniel needs someone to make him jump a little. Both he and his sister are lovely people, despite the damage their parents tried their best to inflict. But they're both so serious minded. Daniel's acted positively middle-aged since he was eighteen."

"That's why he's the perfect employee. He holds me down when I go off on flights of fancy."

"You, Herbert? On flights of fancy? Whatever can you mean?"

"There are people other than Daniel who would question my sanity at pledging so much money to that young woman's school."

"Oh, Herbert." Eugenia rose from her chair. "Would I do anything to risk your money?"

While getting to his feet, he cocked a skeptical eyebrow. "If memory serves me correctly, you gambled away a small fortune of my money at the derby."

"You're right, of course, but I did apologize," she murmured, smiling at that particular memory. Gambling was always more enjoyable when it was done with someone's else money.

Herbert's eyes had narrowed with suspicion. "And after that, you refused all my invitations. That's not going to happen again, is it?"

"Certainly not." Eugenia smiled at him and was rewarded by the mellowing of his baleful expression. Dear me, she thought, the things I do for my girls. However, this had seemed like the perfect way to make sure Cassandra and Daniel *had* to spend some time together. She knew if they weren't forced, the memory of a silly school-days disagreement would keep them apart forever.

Though she'd never known exactly what it was they argued about, their feud had been going on far too long. It wasn't that she believed Daniel and Cassandra should have gotten together when they were so young. No, she was glad they had seen something of the world and of other people. But enough was enough. They should have realized years ago that they belonged together. She would have to push them, just as she had pushed her niece, Liz, into finding romance. And look how wonderfully that had turned out. Liz and Nathan had married in April and were blissfully happy.

Now if all went as smoothly with Daniel and Cassandra, all she'd have left to worry about was Maggie. "Oh, my," Eugenia murmured, thinking about Daniel's younger sister. Maggie was a big worry indeed.

"Is something wrong?" Herbert inquired with gentle courtesy.

Eugenia smiled. He really was a handsome man. Gallant, too, in the way men used to be. If she hadn't sworn there'd never be another after...

Turning purposefully from sad thoughts, she took Herbert's arm. "Now what could be wrong, Herbert? I'm feeling so good that I believe I'll let you take me to lunch. We can drink a toast to Daniel and Cassandra. I just know they're getting along famously by now."

On the sidewalk outside Cassandra's school, Daniel gazed about him in openmouthed wonder. He couldn't believe his eyes.

"So what do you think?" she asked with a proud smile.

Yes, he could believe it, Daniel corrected. After all, this was Cassandra he was dealing with. He took a deep breath and tried to find the words to describe his feelings.

"Daniel?"

He found his voice at last. "Of all your stupid, scatterbrained, idiotic schemes, Cassandra, this one takes first prize."

Her smile disappeared as she planted both her hands on her hips. She looked as infuriated and determined as she'd been at seven years old when he'd told her she couldn't fly off the roof with homemade wings. "And what, pray tell, is wrong with my school?"

Daniel looked once more at the disintegrating pile of brick and mortar that she had called a building. "Mush for brains," he said. "That's what you've always had, Cassandra Diane Martin. Mush for brains."

TWO

"Mush for brains?" Cassandra repeated, eyes widening.

"Just look at this place." Daniel indicated the school building with a sweep of his arm. "You're lucky it hasn't fallen down around you."

"I'll have you know it's structurally sound."

"Who told you that? The con artist who leased it to you?"

Cassandra took a step backward. "He wasn't a con artist. And he *sold* it to me," she added softly.

"What?"

She cleared her throat, but her voice still came out as little more than a whisper. "He sold it to me."

Daniel's face turned red and then white and then red again. Almost like a revolving barber's pole, Cassandra decided nonsensically. Funny how the knowledge that she had purchased this building did that to men's faces. Her father had looked much the same when she'd told him where a chunk of her inheritance from her grandfather had gone. That was the reason her parents weren't speaking to her right now, even though she was living in the same house with them.

"I got a terrific deal on it," she offered after a long pause. When Daniel still didn't say anything, she told him the price.

Ashen faced, he leaned against the side of his car. "Cassandra, why on earth would you do something so ridiculous? Even *you* used to be smarter than this."

She bristled. "Everyone says to invest in real estate."

"Not real estate in this part of town, especially since you're trying to run a school out of this—" he looked at the building as if searching for the right description "—this monstrosity."

Cassandra wheeled back to survey the building. Why couldn't he see how perfect it was? A warehouse in its former life, the building had all the features she had been looking for—plenty of room, a location not too far from the homes and schools of the majority of her pupils. It had taken relatively little work and money to convert the inside into an auditorium and a series of smaller rooms and offices. Even the acoustics were wonderful. So the outside wasn't all that great and the neighborhood not one of Nashville's finest. That wasn't a requirement. She started to tell Daniel the place now looked better than it had six months ago. She reconsidered.

"All it needs is some paint and minor repairs," she said instead. "And the inside is great. You'll see. Come on, I'll give you the grand tour." She took hold of his arm.

"I think I've already seen enough," Daniel retorted, shaking off her hand.

A spark of temper flared through her. "Oh, don't be such a prig."

He blinked at her. "A prig?"

She swallowed a giggle at his startled expression. Heaven only knew where she had come up with the word *prig*, but as he stood beside his square foreign sedan, in his uncreasable suit, Daniel looked too proper to be called anything else. She had known him all her life, and he had always been serious but never implacably somber as he was now. He reminded her of a youthful Ebenezer Scrooge. She could almost see him hunched over a desk, frowning as he counted his money by candlelight. And that wouldn't do at all, she decided. Shoulders as wide and strong and masculine as Daniel's should never hunch. And she couldn't stand to see him frowning so much. Not when she could remember the way golden-brown lights had danced in his eyes when he laughed, the way his sharply handsome features had softened when he had looked at her.

Somewhere inside this stern, older-than-his-years man, there had to be a hint of the Daniel she had known. Perhaps she'd find him if she could just get him to smile.

To that end, she laughed.

Daniel just glared at her. "Cassandra, this isn't a laughing matter. You've thrown a small fortune down the toilet."

"Toilet? Goodness, Daniel, I wouldn't expect someone so proper to talk about something as indelicate as toilets."

"Cassandra—"

"When did you become such a stuffed shirt?"

"It's better than being an impetuous child."

She shook a finger at him. "Daniel, Daniel, don't you remember that I always won in our little name-calling sessions?"

The reply he had been formulating disappeared, and Cassandra took advantage of his discomfiture to pull him toward the building. The casual touch sent an unexpected tingle racing through her. His hand was as she remembered it—large, a bit hard, all male. It was strange how her hand still fit his so perfectly, as if it had been planned that way. The thought disturbed Cassandra, and she drew away from him just inside the school's entrance. She couldn't quite look at his face as she threw open the set of double doors leading to the auditorium.

"It's lunchtime, so nothing's scheduled in here right now," she chattered, full of nerves. "But there's a play rehearsal at three o'clock."

Fighting the unreasonable urge to take her soft hand in his again, Daniel paused in the doorway. From somewhere in the building he could hear singing and the muted sound of a piano. Those sounds were cut off as the door swung shut behind him. He took a deep breath. The room smelled of fresh paint and plaster, and from the look of things, both had been put to recent and good use.

It wasn't what he expected. He admitted that much as he mounted a few shallow steps and stood at the back of the moderate sized auditorium. The floor fell in graduated levels toward the front of the room, where black curtains had been drawn to the sides of a stage. The seats were folding chairs. The carpeting was a practical but attractive blue. All in all, the room was a triumph of economical design. Looking around, he really couldn't fault it.

Not until he noticed the plastered-over cracks in the wall.

Without a word, he walked over, ran a finger down the most obvious crevice and sent Cassandra an eyebrow-raised, knowing glance.

"Oh, pooh!" she said, exactly as he could have predicted. "What are a few little cracks?"

"Sometimes they mean structural instability." Daniel glanced up at the loft that housed the theater's light booth and the ceiling that soared well above that. "Down around your ears," he muttered in an ominous voice.

"The building inspector gave us an okay, and I've got statements from an architect and engineer that say everything is fine."

"They were probably paid off by the real-estate agent."

"I commissioned them myself."

"How reassuring," he said, still looking at the ceiling as if he expected it to crash to the floor at any minute.

"Now just stop it, Daniel. Stop finding fault and look at the good points." Cassandra went down the aisle and up on the stage. At its center, she turned around, throwing her arms wide to encompass the room.

Daniel walked down the aisle at a slower pace, his attention caught by the length of leg revealed by her flaring, short red skirt. Those legs were hard to ignore from this angle below the stage. From any angle, he corrected. Alarmed by the jolt of desire that crackled through him, he shifted his gaze to her vibrant,

smiling face. Wrong move, he decided and looked
away—at the floor, at the ceiling, anywhere but at
Cassandra.

"Isn't it a wonderful room?" she was saying. "Before we even did the renovations, I could imagine the
stage and the seats filled with people. I could see the
plays we could do here. I could smell the greasepaint
and feel the heat from the lights."

He chanced another look up at her, and finding her
eyes closed, he gazed long and hard. It had been some
years since he had allowed himself to really look at
her. Six years to be exact. During a business trip to
New York City, he had impulsively found the obscure
workshop theater where Maggie had told him Cassandra was appearing. He had sat unnoticed in a back
row, mesmerized as always by her talent and her vital-
ity. Afterward he had slipped away, pursued by the
memory of how she had once betrayed him.

Daniel had known about betrayal from a young age,
but he had never expected it from Cassandra. Maybe
that was why the memory continued to throb. Practical man that he was, he didn't waste much time on
senseless regrets or longings. Only when he looked at
her could he still hurt. The feeling was an ache, like an
old injury on a rainy day.

He was aching when Cassandra opened her eyes and
looked into his. The pain sharpened immediately, in-
tensified by his inability to look away.

The vulnerability Cassandra read in Daniel's face
made her pause. At last, she thought, at last he looks
human again. She took a step forward, smiling a little, emboldened as always by being on a stage.

"Daniel, I know you think I'm as irresponsible as I
was when I was twelve, but I'm not." Again she spread

her arms wide. "I love this school. These kids. I love what I'm doing here."

The skepticism started to creep back into his expression, and she quickly tried to stop it. "It's not a whim or a scheme. I just keep remembering how I felt the first time I stepped onto a stage—I knew I had come home. And all through the years, although I've never had any big success, I've never lost that feeling." She shrugged and laughed out loud. "What I want to do is help some kids discover that feeling, too. Can you fault me for that?"

As acquainted as Daniel was with Cassandra's flair for the dramatic, he was still captivated by her little speech. And he couldn't resist her laughter. Not this time. So he grinned.

She executed another turn, her curling dark hair fanning around her. "See, Daniel, I knew you'd understand." She stopped twirling and hugged herself. "Do you remember my first stage appearance? I think you were in the audience."

He nodded, pulled back in time despite his best attempts at resistance. "I was there under great pressure from my grandparents. You and Maggie and Liz were seven or eight."

"In the second-grade spring pageant. Maggie refused to go on at the last minute, and Liz stuck with her."

"You made up for their absence." He chuckled.

A chuckle, Cassandra thought in amazement, a real, honest-to-goodness chuckle. Now he was really thawing. "And I performed my own song."

"Which wasn't on the program."

She laughed again. "Our teacher was flabbergasted, and Mother and Daddy didn't know what to think."

"They never knew what to think about you."

"They never knew what to do with me, period. You know that. They were either telling me I was wonderful or crying about something I'd done to disgrace them." Wryly Cassandra shook her head. "I guess that's what comes from having an unexpected child when you're past forty and all your other kids are teenagers."

"Oh, is that it?"

"My whole family spoiled me shamelessly."

"You're not telling me anything I didn't already know."

She ignored the dryness of his tone. "They encouraged me to be creative, but when I did something unexpected, like writing a song and performing it impromptu, they didn't know how to react." She grinned again. "You know, I believe I still remember that song I sang in that second-grade pageant." Without preamble, Cassandra launched into the simple tune.

Her strong, true alto broke over Daniel like a rainstorm. Husky, undeniably sexy, her mature voice gave new meaning to a childish song about the man in the moon. She sang without self-consciousness, with the passion of someone who sings just for the joy of it. He found it easy to lose himself in her voice, the way he always lost himself in Cassandra.

The warning was sounding inside him, but he ignored it, content for the moment to see where these tender, resurrected feelings might lead.

She ended the song with a flourish and a curtsy, and he applauded on cue. Eyes shining, she gave him another cheeky grin. "Thanks, Daniel."

"I always applaud you."

Her expression sobered a bit. "Yes, but you haven't smiled at me in such a long, long time."

Unaccountably he ducked his head and stared at his feet. He wouldn't have been surprised to see the scuffed toes of a pair of sneakers instead of the smooth leather of his expensive wing tips. For he had felt just this way on the day he'd first noticed that Cassandra was a girl. Not just his sister's friend or his childhood playmate. Not the daughter of his grandparents' next-door neighbor. But a girl. With pert, thrusting breasts and a curvy little behind. With black eyes, shining dark hair and a smile that could make a boy's heart turn over and over and over again.

Memories rocketed through him: the buttery smell of popcorn, hands meeting as if by accident in the darkness of a theater, the strawberry flavor of the lipstick she'd worn the first time they kissed. The simple awe to be felt in watching her onstage.

These were some of Daniel's best memories, the ones he rarely allowed himself to call upon. Now he took a deep breath and let them burst into full color.

Before he could react to his feelings, Cassandra had stepped to the edge of the stage, holding out her arms with the same innocent thrust she might have used fifteen years ago. Her hands came down on his shoulders, his automatically reached to her waist as he swung her to the floor.

The feel of her was almost the same—small and soft and so very feminine. She was so unchanged he thought they might have actually stepped back in time.

The difference was he was no longer a teenager. He was a man, with a man's experience with physical attraction and where it could lead. The experience made it both easier and more difficult to step back from Cassandra.

There was understanding in her gaze. Yet she took his hand again, and held on. His fingers curled around hers. "Come on, Daniel," she invited. "Let's look at the rest of my school."

Her school. The improbable thought of Cassandra with a school made him laugh again, but he followed her from the auditorium with no argument.

He tried his best not to be impressed with what he saw. Like the outside, the rest of the building was a bit ramshackle, but the practice and meeting rooms were comfortable, clean and made cheerful by colorful paint and new carpet. The second-story offices were much the same. Cassandra's sported a window full of plants and a bright red-painted desk. Daniel was reassured by the messiness of that desktop. At least the untidy pile of papers was what he could have predicted.

He didn't intend to spend the day at the school. But he stayed, forgetting everything else that demanded his attention back at the office. He met most of the staff, sat in on an impromptu but surprisingly good jam session in one of the music rooms, and spent hours poring over the school's finances while Cassandra conducted a play rehearsal.

The day was beginning to fade when he laid aside his pencil and stretched, noticing that the clock on Cassandra's desk was thirteen minutes faster than his Swiss-accurate watch. Knowing Cassandra and her tendency to be late, she had probably set it that way.

He grinned, and his stomach growled insistently. It wasn't unusual for him to work through lunch. Today, however, he was so hungry he could actually imagine the smell of food.

"Hungry?"

Daniel glanced up as Cassandra came through the door carrying a picnic basket. "How did you know?"

"You know I'm psychic."

"I do?"

"Remember? When I was ten, I was able to find that brooch my mother had lost."

"Wasn't that really because you and Liz had been playing in her jewelry without permission the day before."

Cassandra rolled her eyes. "You were always so darn honest, Daniel."

"And usually hungry." He pushed away from the desk and stood. "That hasn't changed, either. What have you got in the basket?"

"Uh-uh," she said, pulling it away. "If you want dinner, you have to come upstairs with me."

"I thought we were on the top floor."

"Think again." Behind the door of what he had assumed was a closet, a narrow staircase was revealed. "Let's go up."

It was just like Cassandra to install a small patio on part of the building's flat rooftop. Complete with an umbrellaed table and chairs and a flower box of petunias to scent the air, the tiny retreat offered an undistinguished view of a decaying neighborhood. The day, however, had been a beauty, cooler than normal for June, and now a pleasant breeze was kicking up, promising to make the evening even more enjoyable.

"Sometimes a girl just has to have a place to get away by herself," Cassandra explained. "Terribly frivolous of me, right?"

"I always said you were a frivolous person."

"But I really have learned to curb some of those tendencies."

Not giving voice to his doubts about that, Daniel took the picnic hamper and set it on the table. The woven wood basket was of the type he'd seen advertised in upscale mail-order catalogs for a ridiculous price. Talk about frivolity, he thought. Cassandra opened it, and he expected her to bring out some pasta or pâté, a little fresh fruit and cheese, perhaps some wine of moderately good vintage. That suited his image of the life he imagined she led. He certainly didn't expect the take-out chicken and diet cola she produced instead.

"What's wrong?" she asked, seeing his surprise. "Have you lost your taste for grease or something? I had to go pick this up, you know, while you were immersed in my finances."

"I suppose you bought the hamper while you were out, too?"

"Of course not. I keep it in the car. I never know when I might feel like a picnic."

He laughed. How typical of Cassandra to pack fast food in a pricey hamper and call it a picnic. If she had ever done the predictable, she wouldn't have been Cassandra.

He was still laughing when he sat down. Cassandra took the chair next to his and decided to plunge right in and ask the big question. "So what do you think, Mr. Right-hand Man, would your boss be wasting his money on this worthy cause?"

He took his time answering, first biting into a drumstick, then wiping his mouth on a napkin, then gazing thoughtfully at the horizon. Cassandra was thinking about screaming by the time he answered. "It does look as if you've put a little thought into this place," he said slowly.

That was high praise, considering it came from Daniel. She let her smile beam.

Then he added, "But I have to say—"

She cut him off by clapping a hand over his mouth. "No, no, no. No buts. Not tonight. I've had much too exhausting a day. You can tell me everything I'm doing wrong tomorrow." She lifted her hand from his mouth.

"Cassandra—"

Her hand went back. "Am I going to have to muzzle you?"

There was laughter in his eyes, so she withdrew her hand again. All he did was reach for another piece of chicken. "I am allowed to eat, aren't I?"

"Please do."

They ate for a while in comfortable silence. Amazingly comfortable, Cassandra decided, thinking how pleased Eugenia would be if she could see them now. Cassandra was going to have to talk to the woman about the little trick she had pulled, but perhaps it was working out okay. At least Daniel had warmed up a bit. And that was all Cassandra wanted. Once upon a time, he had been her champion. Then, after that long-ago summer night, he had tried to be less than nothing to her. She much preferred to think the coming years would include having him as a friend.

Lost in such pleasant thoughts, she didn't quite catch what Daniel was asking her. "Pardon?"

"I was wondering when you got your college degree."

She took a long sip of her drink. "How did you know about that?"

"It's listed on some papers I looked over today."

Shrugging, she reached for another piece of chicken. "It only took me about eight years, in between everything else I was doing."

"College doesn't fit my image of you as a free spirit."

For some reason the remark irritated her. "Has it ever occurred to you that your image of me is based on someone I stopped being years ago?"

He considered her for a moment, then shook his head. "People don't change that much, Cassandra. That's why I—"

"Now you promised," she cut in. "You promised not to criticize me until tomorrow."

"I did?"

"Yes, and I'm holding you to it." After a last bite of chicken, she swept her scraps up in a plastic wrapper and dumped them into the picnic hamper. "If you're finished, you can take me to a movie I need to see."

"A movie? Now wait a minute—"

"A friend of mine is in it," she continued, taking his box of chicken away. "It's one of those slasher things—*Subway Nightmares* or something like that."

"I'm not going to see one of those teenage bloodbaths." Though she reached for his half-empty cola bottle, Daniel snatched it away.

"Would you rather I went by myself?" Not pausing for his reply, she sighed in resignation. "Okay, but if some hormone-ravaged teen is inspired by the movie to slit my throat in the parking lot, I know you're going to feel guilty."

It was Cassandra's talent that she could make such preposterous predictions sound so possible. Her talent or my gullibility, Daniel thought an hour or so later as the blood splattered from the movie's fifth nubile victim. He winced and reached for some of Cassandra's popcorn. She reached at the same time, and their hands collided. The feeling was familiar and decidedly disconcerting.

He tried hard to concentrate on the screen, all too aware of the gentle pressure of Cassandra's arm against his own. "Is your friend dead yet?" he whispered.

"My friend is the crazy guy."

Eyes narrowing, Daniel watched the movie's requisite psychopath swing his double-edged ax with convincing fury. "How well do you know this person?"

"He was one of my roommates for a while."

A kernel of corn lodged in Daniel's throat. *One* of her roommates? The vision that sprang to his mind wasn't pretty.

As if sensing his thoughts, she patted his arm. "It's okay. There were five of us sharing the place at the time."

Not reassured, he coughed, and Cassandra's laughter bubbled over, earning them a chorus of shushes from nearby teens who were intent on the film. Sliding down in his seat, Daniel kept further comments to himself until they were heading through the parking lot.

"That guy was really a roommate?"

"He's a terrific actor. We did *Romeo and Juliet* at a Shakespeare festival a few years back. There was a mix-up on accommodations, and a half dozen of us had to share a cabin. It was chaotic and very platonic.''

Telling himself he didn't really care if it had been platonic or not, Daniel held the car door open for her. "If this guy is so good, why's he doing a trash movie like this?"

"Trash pays. Even terrific actors need to eat." Cassandra laughed up at him, and Daniel caught his breath. Light from the street lamp above spilled over her, framing her face, tipping her long, curling lashes with gold. What a beautiful face, Daniel thought, enchanted by the picture she presented. He barely resisted the urge to touch the soft curve of her cheek and stepped back. A curious sense of déjà vu settled over him.

With that feeling so strong, it was easy to take the familiar road to her parents' home, to park in the semicircular driveway, to walk with Cassandra toward the house. Lights were burning on either side of the door, attracting a furious swarm of insects. Mrs. Martin's prized roses climbed a trellis at one end of the broad front porch. Daniel drew in their scent. The feelings the smell evoked were strange. They confused him. Especially as he gazed into Cassandra's dark eyes. He was in the present. And in the past, too. He had been here with her a hundred times. And yet never before.

As he dwelled on the conflicting impressions, she slipped her hands into his. If he stepped just a fraction closer, her lips would be under his, her body pressed tight to his own. It would all be so familiar. But so new. His arms slipped around her, drawing her close, until her own rich, faintly exotic fragrance replaced the scent of the flowers. His heart began to pound. Or was that her heart? It was hard to tell.

Her chuckle was low and somewhat shaky. Her voice breathless. "It's crazy, isn't it? It just seemed so natural for you to bring me home that I forgot my car is at the school."

Daniel frowned at that piece of reality. The school. Her school. It was a little like focusing the lens of a camera, but everything became very clear. He had to remind himself of what day it was, even what year it was. And then he realized how close he was to kissing Cassandra.

And, by God, he couldn't do that.

Smothering a curse, he backed away. She stared up at him with a mixture of surprise and regret. "Daniel?"

Still trying to chase the fog of the past from his brain, he shook his head. "I just realized what's been happening. You took over my whole day."

"Took over?"

"Completely."

"I didn't force you to stay with me."

But you did, he wanted to insist. The only force she'd needed was her smile. That, and a foolish little song she'd written when she was eight. From that moment on, he'd been out of his head, a lump of clay ready to do her bidding.

He had to remember to avoid that smile. At all costs.

"I've got to go," he muttered, glancing at his watch. "I left a desk full of work. I missed an appointment." He glared at her. "And a racquetball game."

So that's how he keeps the hard body, Cassandra thought as she began to smile.

"I play racquetball every Tuesday and Thursday," he continued. "My partner must think I've been kidnapped or something."

Cassandra tried very hard to suppress her giggle, but it was difficult with Daniel looking as if he'd been placed under a spell.

Finally giving voice to an extremely rude and graphic oath, he turned on his heel and left. In a moment she heard the engine of his car spring to life, and the wheels squealed a little as he tore out of the driveway.

The front door opened then, and her mother stepped out. Maybe I have gone back to the past, Cassandra thought, giving in to the laughter welling up inside her. Her mother had always come out to make sure she and Daniel didn't spend too much time necking on the front porch.

"Cassandra?" her mother said, obviously forgetting that she hadn't spoken to her youngest daughter in a week. "What are you doing out here?"

"I was talking to Daniel."

The amazement came, just as Cassandra had known it would. "Daniel O'Grady?"

"No, Daniel Boone," she teased as she pressed a kiss on her mother's plump but still pretty cheek. A disapproving sniff followed her across the foyer and up the stairs. Her father came out of his study, demanding to know what was going on. Cassandra paused on the top step, heard Daniel's name and the expected groan. She giggled some more and decided it was a good thing she was looking for a place of her own.

But thoughts of Daniel crowded everything else aside. In her room, she hugged the knowledge to her chest. She still could make him forget everything but her. Why that realization made her feel so triumphant she couldn't really say, but she couldn't wait to share it with Liz. And Maggie, too. Of all people, Maggie knew how stuffy her brother could be. Today's events would give her a chuckle.

Daniel. Cassandra kicked off her shoes and said his name aloud. Just the sound of it sent a tingle down her spine.

About midnight Daniel finally admitted he wasn't getting any work done. Grumbling to himself, he locked up the offices and started to leave.

Wally, the night security guard, called a friendly greeting down from the hall before Daniel could press the elevator call button. He and the older man knew each other. They had commiserated often over a late-night cup of coffee.

"Finally packing it in?" Wally asked.

"Yeah." Daniel punched the button with more than the necessary force and ran a hand along his unshaven jaw. "There's fresh coffee made in our offices. I just shut off the machine."

"Thanks." Wally peered at him closely. "You all right, Mr. O'Grady?"

So it's that obvious that I'm losing my mind, Daniel thought, grinning despite himself. "I got problems, Wally."

"Female involved?" At Daniel's nod, the man shook his head and heaved a sympathetic sigh. "Go home, Mr. O'Grady. Sleep on it. By morning, you'll probably have decided she's not worth the worry."

That would be nice, Daniel decided as he got on the elevator and waved goodbye to the guard. But he already knew Cassandra wasn't worth the worry, and it didn't help the way he was feeling.

At his apartment, he tossed his jacket aside, poured himself some Scotch and flipped on the television, switching the channels until he found the talk-show host who could usually make him laugh. Not tonight, though. Instead, he turned down the volume and started going through his bookshelf, looking for the photo album his sister had insisted he take when they had divided their parents' things.

It was on the bottom shelf, almost hidden among some weighty college economics textbooks. Daniel settled down in the chair, took a long sip of his drink and opened the first page. His parents' picture smiled up at him. His finger automatically traced over his mother's pretty face. His parents were both so very young here. So happy. Not at all the way he remembered them.

Trying to blunt the beginnings of the usual bitterness, he drank a little more Scotch and flipped through the pages until he found the picture he really wanted. He found it and promptly drained his glass.

It was his senior prom picture. His hair had been so long then, almost skimming his shoulders, as foolish looking to him now as the navy blue tux. Navy blue? Daniel laughed. Why had Cassandra insisted on blue? Her dress had been white. He sobered as he stared down at her beautiful, young, innocent face.

Then he shut the album with a little bang and reached for the phone.

Three

Cassandra pulled out the wicker-backed restaurant chair and smiled at the two women already seated at the table. "Hi, guys. Sorry I'm late." Her friends looked at each other and laughed. "What did I do?" Cassandra demanded, sitting down.

"You apologized for being late." Grinning, Liz signaled for a waitress.

"When you're always late," Maggie added.

Cassandra sighed as she shrugged out of her white linen jacket. The sun-splashed atrium of their favorite restaurant was warm this afternoon. "I'm getting better, though, don't you think?"

"Oh, definitely." Liz patted her arm. "You got here before we were ready for coffee this time. I believe that's a record."

All three of them shared a comfortable laugh while the waitress appeared and put a spinach salad in front of Cassandra. "Your friends ordered for you," she explained.

"And what if I had wanted something else?"

"We've been coming here for ten years," Maggie said. "And you've never wanted anything else."

"You're right." Cassandra dismissed the waitress with a smile and dug into the crumbled-bacon-and-mushroom-topped salad. She really didn't care what she ate. Other than the school, spending time with Liz and Maggie was what she liked most about having moved home to Nashville. Eagerly they caught up on one another's lives, speaking in the special abbreviated language of friends who had known each other forever.

They got together as often as their busy schedules would allow, at Eugenia's for tea or with just the three of them for lunch or dinner. Cassandra knew the way their friendship had endured was something special, especially considering the changes they had all been through. She had moved away. Maggie had lost a child, divorced and, to everyone's surprise, had become one of the city's most sought-after interior designers. Liz had finally taken time from her law career and her charitable causes to find romance. The diamonds in her wedding band were flashing as she gestured, explaining in great detail a farfetched story her husband had told her about a local politician.

"If Nathan told you that, it just proves that men like to gossip, too," Cassandra said.

Liz's blue eyes sparkled. "Especially when they're in public relations and they have a wife whose curiosity is insatiable."

"But what happens when the wife's friends tell everyone in town?"

"That's easy," Maggie put in, giggling. "The PR man then denies everything."

"And denying rumors is really what public relations firms are good for," Liz pointed out. "So gossip from a PR man is really part of a self-perpetuating cycle."

Cassandra speared a last spinach leaf and smiled. "Nathan might not like the way you talk about his profession."

"Nathan adores me," Liz said with the confidence of a woman in love. "And, therefore, I can speak my mind about everything."

"A perfectly balanced, mutually supportive relationship." Maggie brushed a lock of blond hair from her cheek and propped her chin in hand. "Liz, I hope you realize you have exactly what everyone's looking for."

Cassandra put down her fork. "Speaking of relationships—"

"Yes," Liz cut in, looking at Maggie. "Speaking of them. How is Don?"

Maggie's sigh was pure bliss. Her brown eyes, so like her brother's, crinkled at the corners as she smiled. "Don is just wonderful. We're going out of town this weekend."

While their friend was dreamy eyed, Liz and Cassandra traded long-suffering glances. Everyone except Maggie thought Don was a boring fuddy-duddy. A financial planner, his main topics of conversation were stocks and bonds. Unless of course one could get him to reverse the order and talk about bonds and stocks. He was exactly the sort of solid, dependable type Maggie had been drawn to since her divorce, but it seemed to Cassandra, and to Liz and Eugenia, that she could find someone a bit more exciting.

"And speaking of excitement," Cassandra said, following her train of thought instead of the conversation.

Liz blinked in confusion. "Were we speaking of excitement?"

"We are now." Ever dramatic, Cassandra paused, looking from one friend to the other. "Guess who I spent yesterday with."

"Daniel," Liz and Maggie said in unison.

"How did you know? Eugenia?" Cassandra demanded, deflated.

"Well, she told me," Liz admitted. "But—"

"—I heard it from Daniel," Maggie completed.

"Daniel told you? What did he say?" Cassandra heard the breathless tone of her voice and saw the look that passed between her friends. She bit her lip and managed what she hoped was a nonchalant shrug. "There's no reason why he shouldn't have told you. It was just business, although Eugenia probably said it was something else."

Liz took a compact from her purse and smoothed a curling tendril of chestnut hair into the already neat bun at the nape of her neck. "Been a while since you and Daniel spent any time together, hasn't it?" she commented with the utmost casualness.

"Well, it was just business," Cassandra repeated, wondering why she was trying to emphasize that.

"Business?" A tiny frown drew Maggie's eyebrows together as she reached for her glass of iced tea.

Cassandra waited in vain for her to continue, but she seemed absorbed in her drink. "Well," Cassandra finally prompted her. "Aren't you going to tell me exactly what Daniel said?"

"He mentioned something about the school."

"And?"

"And he said you spent the day together."

"Blast it, Maggie, get to the point," Cassandra said in irritation. "I don't care if he is your brother, you have to tell me everything he said."

"To tell you the truth I can hardly remember."

"Can't remember?"

"It was about one o'clock in the morning when he called."

"One?" Cassandra repeated. Now why in the world had Daniel called his sister at that time of night to talk about her? And what else had he said?

Before Cassandra could pursue the matter, Liz glanced at her watch. "Golly, I didn't realize it was so late. Sorry to break this up, but I've got to be in court in half an hour."

It could have been Cassandra's imagination, but she thought the smile Maggie sent Liz's way was a bit conspiratorial. Whatever the case, Maggie also picked up her purse and prepared to leave. "I have to be going, too. I'm supposed to meet a client all the way across town."

"But you can't leave now," Cassandra protested.

"Aren't you finished with lunch?" Maggie asked.

"Yes, but—"

"Then I've got to run," Liz said, picking up their check. "Isn't it my turn to get this?" She put some money on the table and smiled at her friends. "Let's do this again. Soon."

"Call me," Maggie murmured to Cassandra, turning to wave as she followed Liz through the crowded restaurant.

Cassandra stayed where she was for a moment or two, amazed at the deftness with which she had been abandoned. Then she got to her feet, dragging her jacket on as she hurried after her friends. She had to dodge a waiter with a loaded tray, however, and got to the parking lot just in time to see Liz's and Maggie's cars leave.

Muttering to herself, she slipped on her favorite black-and-white polka-dotted sunglasses and stalked to her white MG. Once inside, she turned the ignition and revved the engine. A blond hunk paused on the sidewalk to send her and the car an admiring glance. But for once Cassandra didn't flirt. She was too irritated. So irritated she tore out of the parking lot on squealing tires.

Some friends she had, hiding what Daniel had said about her. Of course, Maggie might have just been trying to spare her feelings. Daniel might have said something incredibly nasty about her, just as he'd done several times through the years. But if he'd said the same old things, why had he waited until one in the morning to do so?

And why, pray tell, was he waiting in the entrance hall when she got to the school?

How very interesting, Cassandra thought as she slipped her glasses down her nose and studied him over the tops. "Hey, sailor," she teased impulsively. "You lookin' for me?"

Her reward was the hastily banked, but unmistakable fire that sparked in his eyes. One thing was for certain. Daniel might still be saying nasty things about her to his sister, but he could no longer pretend to be indifferent. Cassandra wasn't going to let him.

The padded back of the folding chair was amazingly comfortable, Daniel decided. It had to be the chair, because he couldn't admit it was Cassandra who had held him spellbound for the past two hours.

Showing up unannounced at the school this afternoon had been an impulse, but once here he had intended to discuss the endowment with her and leave. Quickly. Without allowing himself to be distracted by her smile. Or her feminine curves. Or the disturbing memories she forced him to examine.

But as usual, nothing worked out as planned when Cassandra was involved. She had an acting workshop scheduled, and he let himself be talked into staying to watch. He hadn't counted on the Cassandra he would discover here.

She was a great teacher. A natural. Not anything he would have expected.

Her students were teenagers, almost a dozen, who had been separated into groups of two or three at an earlier session and were now being asked to perform a scene. The scenes were classics, ranging from the light comedy of Neil Simon's *Sweet Charity* to the pathos of Lillian Hellman's *The Little Foxes*.

Cassandra made herself part of the class, performing with a slender young man who was so nervous they had to begin twice. Once they got started, however, her skill made even his amateurish methods look good. When they were finished, she went over the scene step-by-step, explaining why she had used a particular gesture, how she had internalized the character and played to the audience at the same time.

One by one the students performed their scenes, and one by one their performances were praised, criticized, analyzed. Cassandra used kindness mixed with humor and discipline to get her point across and keep the class moving. The hours could have been boring, especially to a group of teens on a summer afternoon. Yet it was obvious to Daniel that they wanted to be here. It was even more obvious that Cassandra had what it took to keep them fascinated.

This was a side of her he'd never seen before, a world apart from the irresponsible, flighty young woman she usually appeared to be. Maybe, just maybe, she had grown up a little. Last night on the phone, Maggie had told him Cassandra had changed. He hadn't believed her, but he couldn't argue with what he saw here today.

When the class had been dismissed, she walked slowly down the aisle to the back row where he sat. Daniel got to his feet. "I'm impressed," he admitted with some reluctance. "I didn't plan to be, but I am."

"It was just a typical workshop."

"Though I don't know much about what's typical, I'd say this was a little more than that."

Grinning, she picked her jacket up from the chair where she'd thrown it before the class. "They're such great kids. So eager to learn. Working with them gives me a rush that's almost as good as an opening night."

"Just almost?"

"Yes, but damn close."

Daniel sat down again, sighing.

"Uh-oh." Cassandra took the chair in front of his, propping her legs on an adjoining seat as she turned to face him. "That sigh had an ominous ring to it."

With her mouth fixed in such a pretty pout, she looked about ten. Her clinging purple sundress belied her youthful expression, however, and Daniel had to remind himself not to think of her as the sexy woman he had been a fraction of an inch away from kissing last night. They had to talk seriously about her school. "I can't help wishing the school gave you just as good a feeling as performing," he said.

"Why?"

"Because maybe then I'd be convinced you were going to stick with this."

Thoughtfully she twirled a long strand of hair around her finger and gazed at the ceiling. Daniel would have given a great deal now to know what was going on in her head.

"Did you talk Mr. Black out of the endowment?" she asked, finally breaking the long silence.

He shook his head. "I think you know that your funds are guaranteed. Eugenia's made certain of that. I'm here, going through the motions of checking you out because I happen to care how my boss's money is spent."

"And you think this won't last."

He shrugged. "All I can say is it would be a shame if it turned out to be another of your whims. A lot of people would be disappointed. Your students. Your staff." *And me,* he started to add before catching himself. *No, what he thought of her couldn't matter. For it wouldn't do to give Cassandra the power to disappoint him again.* "There's Eugenia, too, you know," he continued. "She's gone to bat for you in a big way."

Cassandra's mouth tightened at that. "You know what? Much as I appreciate her help, I sort of wish I could have proven myself to your boss on my own."

Now she had truly surprised Daniel. The girl he had once known had often chosen the easy path, the one paved for her by indulgent parents, admiring teachers and good friends. That girl had become a woman who flitted from venture to venture, never sticking with anything long enough to make it work. But that person didn't quite jive with the determination he could now read in her face.

While he studied her, she leaned forward, her soft hand catching his in a fierce grip. "Please, Daniel," she began. "I want you to—"

The doors to the auditorium burst open behind them, cutting off what she might have said. They both turned to watch an angry boy barrel down the aisle, pursued by a young woman Daniel recognized as Nora Cummings, the counselor Cassandra had introduced him to yesterday.

"Oh, no, not again," Cassandra murmured before dropping Daniel's hand and getting up. "Matt?" she called, hurrying after the child.

He ignored her, kicked at a chair and sent an entire row of folding seats crashing to the floor. Cassandra reached for his shoulder, and he wheeled around, kicking another chair with such force that Daniel started forward, ready to intervene.

"Matt, stop it!" Cassandra said with the same firmness she had used earlier with the acting class. "Whatever it is that's bothering you, tearing up the place won't help."

"I don't want to talk to her." The boy's angry voice echoed through the auditorium as he pointed at Nora.

"All she wants to talk about is Dad. And he's dead. So why do I have to talk about him?"

Bitterness is never pretty to look at, Daniel thought. He had watched it grow in his parents' eyes long enough to know how it twisted and maimed. And bitterness from a child is a particularly potent acid, easily recognizable to someone who had suffered from its burn. In Matt, Daniel instantly saw a fellow sufferer.

"You asked to talk to me, Matt," the counselor was saying. "And we've talked about your father before—"

"Well, I don't want to talk about him ever again."

"Okay." Nora took a step forward. "Then let's go talk about something else."

He shook his head, but the sneakered foot he swung against a nearby chair wasn't propelled by fury. As if wrung out by his anger, he let his shoulders slump. "I want to talk to Miss Martin. She's who I was really looking for."

Nora looked uncertain, but Cassandra reassured her with more confidence than Daniel felt. Obviously reluctant, Nora left, and Cassandra nodded toward the front row of chairs. "Want to sit down up here, Matt?"

For the first time the boy looked at Daniel. Blue eyes regarded him with open hostility. "Who's he?"

"An old friend of mine," Cassandra explained.

The puppy dog devotion on the boy's face was as clear as the coppery smudge of freckles across his nose. "You're not so old," he told her.

She laughed. "I guess that means you're the old one, Daniel." Quickly she made the introductions, treating the boy with the same courtesy she would give an adult.

That's her secret, Daniel decided as he gravely shook Matt's hand. She gave the kids the same respect she expected in return.

She gestured toward the chairs again. "You have something you want to talk to me about, Matt?"

"No." The boy shoved a hand through his tousled auburn hair. "I just..." Once more he eyed Daniel.

"You want to talk in private?"

Daniel found himself strangely reluctant to leave Cassandra alone with this boy. He was a husky fellow, and if what he'd done to the chairs was any indication, he had a violent streak.

But Matt didn't insist on privacy. He shrugged instead. "I just had a fight with my mom. It was my fault. It doesn't matter."

Cassandra hesitated a moment, studying him. "You sure?"

"Yeah." Again the toe of Matt's sneaker pushed at a chair while his head lowered. "I'm sorry about kicking stuff around."

"Apology accepted."

He looked back at Cassandra, eager now to please. "I'll put the chairs back."

"How about if you go apologize to Mrs. Cummings instead?"

He seemed ready to resist until a smile edged the frown from his face. "You think she might help me memorize my lines?"

Cassandra glanced at her watch. "It's getting kind of late, but she might give you a hand for a while."

Matt was gone in a flash, his mood having shifted like quicksilver.

"His lines?" Daniel repeated when the doors had banged shut.

With a tired sigh, Cassandra sank down into a front-row chair. "Matt's got a part in one of the high-school kids' productions. We needed a precocious twelve-year-old. He was a natural."

Daniel sat down beside her. "He's obviously one of the reasons you've got Nora on staff."

Cassandra nodded and proceeded to explain. "Matt's father died last year. His mother has all she can do to keep food on the table for him and his older brother." She leaned forward, pressing her fingers against the headache that had begun to throb in her temples. "Matt's extremely bright, and the counselor at his school told Nora he was never a problem until the past few months. Lately, he's taken to throwing these little fits of violence."

"It isn't easy for a boy to lose his father."

"I know. And coming here has helped. The acting classes and the play have given him an outlet for his anger and his emotions." Cassandra straightened. "But they think Matt's problems are more than missing his father. Child abuse was suspected at one point."

Daniel's face darkened. "His mother?"

The idea was no less abhorrent to Cassandra. Propelled by anger, she got up and paced in front of the stage, considering the possibilities of what Matt might have been through. "Nothing has been proven," she muttered. "It's not as if Matt's covered in bruises or anything. And as much as he and his mother argue, he will never say a word against her. You heard him today, saying everything was his fault. He loves her, and she's all he has left."

"Then why suspect anything?"

"He writes these poems." She shivered and rubbed her bare arms. "They're so dark. So full of pain and self-loathing." She looked helplessly at Daniel, her eyes filled with hurt. "Why would a boy write something like that?"

Why, indeed? Daniel asked himself, even though he could have given her some possible answers. Cassandra already knew those answers anyway. She knew a great deal about what had happened in the house where Daniel had grown up. That knowledge seemed to hang in the air between them, charging the atmosphere. She took a step forward.

Daniel got to his feet, trying to resist the tug of memories her velvety eyes evoked. "You're getting in deep with this kid. Be careful."

"I just don't want him to hurt so much."

"He's lucky that you care." *As lucky as I was.* The words were there, almost as though Daniel had spoken them aloud, and the need to touch her was suddenly so fierce he clenched his hands into fists. He wouldn't, couldn't give in to that impulse.

"It's not fair," Cassandra whispered. He wondered if she was still talking about Matt or if the statement applied to him.

"What's not fair?"

"Him...us..." Her shoulders sagged, and she whirled away, but not before he saw the glimmer of tears in her eyes.

Tears from Cassandra didn't seem likely, but Daniel reacted to them just the same. Almost before he could think, he was beside her, turning her into his arms, trying to comfort her. Comforting Cassandra came as naturally to him as breathing. "Come on,

Cass. Don't." She looked up at him, blinking away the tears.

"I'm sorry," she whispered. "I'm not usually so—"

"I know. You never cry, at least you never used to."

Never when you could see me, Cassandra said to herself as she struggled to get herself under control. She hated acting so weak. "I think you're right. I'm getting in too deep with Matt."

"It's hard to keep your distance." For Daniel, the words had a double meaning. Seemingly of its own volition, his hand lifted to her hair, smoothing it back from one temple. Strange how so simple an action could set his blood to pumping as it did. His arms tightened around her.

Cassandra let one hand slip up his arm to his shoulder. A boy's muscles had become those of a man. He was strong. And warm. Always so warm. Her hand moved from his shoulder to cup the back of his neck. His hair was shorter but still as soft as she remembered.

"Cass..." His whisper was lost against her mouth, and Daniel knew a moment's regret at having succumbed. But that was just a moment. Then he was drawn under by the torrent of feelings pushing through him. God, what strength these feelings had, fueled by the sweet taste of her lips, the sultry scent of her perfume, the ripened shape of her woman's body. His reacted to the contact. Quickly. Sharply.

When he at last drew away, Daniel waited for sanity to return as it had last night. He tried to tell himself he was drawn to a memory. But the woman in his arms was flesh and blood. Very real. Very desirable.

And the man in him wanted her in ways the boy hadn't known to dream of.

She held on to him, fingers tightening on the lapels of his jacket as her fathomless black eyes looked deep into his. "It's not fair, Daniel. When you kiss me, I shouldn't feel it clear to the soles of my feet. No one else ever made me feel it that way."

Uncaring of what she had revealed about herself and her feelings for him, Cassandra lifted her lips to his again.

Four

Stay here while I get the lights," Daniel murmured, leaving the door to his condominium open as he brushed past Cassandra.

She paused just inside the doorway and let her eyes adjust to the dim light. The afternoon had grown increasingly cloudy, and the fading sunshine outdoors provided little illumination, even after Daniel opened the vertical blinds that covered a wall of glass at the end of the room. He switched on one lamp and then another, but Cassandra stayed where she was, surveying the sleek and contemporary space Daniel now called home.

"Something wrong?"

Cassandra swung her gaze up to meet his. He was frowning, just as he'd done ever since pulling away from their second kiss.

Second kiss? The thought almost made her laugh out loud. She had kissed Daniel hundreds of times, times when he was eager for those kisses. But not today. Today he had backed away. She had been expecting him to leave, when instead he had issued a rather terse invitation to dinner. Now why was that, she wondered? Most likely he was going to spend the evening explaining to her all the reasons why they shouldn't be kissing. And if that was the case, what was she doing here? She'd long ago had her fill of Daniel O'Grady's rejection.

"Cass?" he said now, his frown growing deeper as he stepped toward her.

Realizing she had been staring at him in silence, Cassandra murmured, "I'm fine," closed the door and put away her misgivings. It was good that she was here. She and Daniel had been needing to talk—really talk—for a long time.

"You've got quite a place," she commented as she laid her jacket and purse on a soft zebra-striped chair. A small matching rug was stretched in front of a red-and-black-tiled fireplace. She tapped the rug with the toe of her shoe. "Is this fake, or have you become a big-game hunter?"

His laugh sounded forced, but it was better than his ever-present look of gloom and doom. "Maggie did the decorating, and she assures me the rug's a fake, even though you couldn't tell by the price." He dropped his jacket over a desk chair and headed across the room. "How about a soft drink or something? I've got beer or wine or something harder if you like."

"Wine would be good." He disappeared into what she assumed was the kitchen. Cassandra wandered around the room, testing the comfort of the square gray leather sofa and eyeing the big-screen television and state-of-the-art stereo equipment.

It wasn't difficult to imagine Daniel relaxing here. Newspapers were stacked in an untidy pile by the couch. The latest tell-all book by an ex-government official was open on the low coffee table, and a tie was draped on the swivel arm of a desk lamp. She got up and touched the tie, noticing how the gray stripes blended with the room's decor. The tie he was wearing now wasn't very different, either. Every part of Daniel's life appeared to be very well coordinated, a far cry from the harum-scarum way his parents had raised him and Maggie.

He came from the kitchen then, catching her with the tie in hand. It was silly to be so uncomfortable, but holding an article of his clothing made her feel, somehow, as if she were intruding. Quickly she put the tie down and accepted the chilled glass he offered. "Why is it men have such a hard time hanging up their ties?"

"I don't usually," Daniel said. "But last night . . ." He paused, remembering it was preoccupation with her that had caused his carelessness last night.

He turned away and took a long, tasteless sip from the bottle of beer he held. God, but this was awkward. After that kiss, what could have possessed him to ask her to dinner? He was certain the kiss and what Cassandra had said afterward were merely in reaction to some shared memories. And he knew their past was better left buried. Certainly he'd be better off if he stayed away from Cassandra and those memories. But she had looked so hurt when he'd pulled away. He had felt responsible for the hurt, and stupidly he had said the first thing that had popped into his mind, and invited her to dinner.

Maybe he hadn't really thought she would accept. But she had. And now he felt about as comfortable as a prisoner on an executioner's platform.

And Cassandra's words cut the uncomfortable silence with all the subtlety of a guillotine's blade. "We're going to have to talk about it sooner or later, you know."

Turning back to her, Daniel loosened his suddenly too-tight tie, muttering a lame, "Talk about what?"

"About what's going on between us." Her small chin lifted, as if in challenge. "About that kiss."

"Nothing's going on," he said quickly. "The kiss was nothing."

"Nothing." Cassandra's eyes widened. "Excuse me, but I was there, remember? That kiss didn't feel like nothing."

"It felt like two people who have a history," Daniel insisted, hoping the act of saying the words out loud would make him really believe them. "You were upset about that boy's problems, and I reacted the same way I would have years ago. You and I have been together a lot, and it's brought back some memories. I was just comforting you. That's all it was. I'm sorry—"

"Wait a minute," she interrupted. "If you were just comforting me, why are you apologizing?"

"Because . . ." Daniel faltered for an answer, took another swig of beer and avoided her eyes. "Come on, Cass, let's just forget it, all right?"

Her gaze was skeptical. "You're forgetting it?"

"Of course." The words came easy, but he knew it was going to be a long time before he forgot the feel of

Cassandra's lips beneath his own. After all, even twelve years hadn't been long enough to erase the feelings he'd once had for her. But that was another issue, one he would consider after he got through this evening. She couldn't see that having her there bothered him. He had to be cool, very collected, very calm.

"So," he said with studied casualness, "I hope you like steak."

"Steak?"

"For dinner."

"We've having dinner?"

He gritted his teeth in frustration. "I invited you for dinner, remember? But if you don't want to stay..."

"You certainly don't sound as if you want me to stay. Why did you even invite me?"

Why, indeed? Daniel asked himself yet again. He cleared his throat and attempted a believable explanation. "Cassandra, we're friends—"

"We are?"

"Well, we used to be," he snapped. "And maybe it's time we were again." *Lord, but he was digging himself into a trench. He couldn't be Cassandra's friend.*

She sipped her drink, her dark eyes narrowing with suspicion as she swallowed. "You never wanted to be friends before now. Ever since that night when we..." She paused, searching for the right word. "Ever since we had that misunderstanding—"

"I wouldn't call it that."

"All right, call it whatever you want, but ever since then, you've done everything in your power to avoid me. You wouldn't listen when I tried to explain or when Maggie tried, or even Liz, and you've always thought Liz had good sense. You—"

"You're right," he cut in, unwilling to rehash their ancient history. "I acted like a jerk. Can we leave it at that?"

"But now, after twelve years you've decided not to be a jerk?"

Daniel groaned in frustration. "Dammit, Cassandra, we're adults now. What happened when we were children—"

"We weren't children."

"All right, what happened when we were *younger and less mature* is over and done with. Don't you think it's time we just let it go?"

She studied him in silence. Then she answered in a small, very soft voice. "I would have let it go a long time ago."

"Well, good," he said tightly. "Finally we're both in agreement. Now why don't we just have some dinner and then—"

"I can get the hell out of here?" Cassandra supplied.

"I didn't say that."

"But you thought it." She stepped closer and touched the loosened knot of his tie. He flinched. She smiled. "Do I make you nervous or something, Daniel?"

He schooled his expression to give nothing away. "Don't be silly."

She looked up at him, eyes wide and dark, her mouth just a movement away from his. She moistened her lips, and Daniel felt the perspiration bead on his forehead. But he didn't move. He was determined not to let her see how she affected him. "So," she continued. "If I kissed you now, it wouldn't mean anything. Is that what you're trying to tell me?"

"That's right," Daniel replied, surprised that his voice could sound so steady when his heart was beating in double time. Cassandra moved a little closer, and he fought the urge to step backward. His body had hardened into one continuous ache, but he could control that if she stood right where she was. If she kissed him, however, only divine intervention could save him. Daniel gripped his bottle of beer and steeled himself to make a display of indifference. Cassandra put one hand against his chest. Her touch seemed to burn right through his shirt. Praying hard for strength, Daniel closed his eyes.

Then neither of them moved.

Seconds ticked by like hours before Daniel opened his eyes. Cassandra was staring at him with something akin to guilt. She drew in a deep breath and spun away so quickly the ends of her long dark hair whispered across the cotton of his shirt. He was left swaying a little, with only a trace of her fragrance to remind him of how close they had been.

In front of the window, she turned to face him. "I'm sorry, Daniel. That was very stupid of me."

Frowning, he moved forward. She backed farther away, sending the window blinds jangling along their chain guides. The awkwardness of her movement, so unlike Cassandra's usual grace, made him stop.

"I'm so silly," she rushed on. "I don't know why I just did what I did. I mean, all I've wanted for years now is to know that you were my friend. I wanted our friendship back. I accepted a long time ago that there was nothing else between us."

Nothing else, Daniel repeated silently. Strange how those words landed with such dull finality inside him.

And why? What she said was the truth. It was what
he'd been telling himself, even after they had kissed.

He remained silent while Cassandra took a deep
breath. If possible, Daniel thought, her eyes grew even
darker than normal when she continued. "What I
wanted was for you to like me again, and here was my
chance. You know, with us sort of working together
and all." She blinked and bit her lip. "But, no, I had
to ruin it. I don't know what I was thinking of—saying the things I did, coming on like some kind of
vamp. I'm sorry, I—"

"Cass," he broke in. "Cass, it's okay. It's nothing." *There's absolutely nothing substantial to the
feelings I'm having right now,* he reassured himself.

"Nothing," Cassandra echoed and took another
deep, calming breath. Both of them kept saying this
was nothing. So maybe she should start believing it.
Perhaps she had imagined that spark of attraction.
Perhaps it really was just history. Perhaps the power
of the kiss they'd shared had been only wishful thinking on her part.

"I'm sorry," she said again. "I guess you think I'm
pretty crazy, don't you?"

"You've always been crazy," Daniel replied, and
forced himself to smile.

The softening of his features brought a lump to
Cassandra's throat. He had always been more handsome, more approachable when he smiled, and she
had always been the one who could coax those grins
from him. He could be stern and filled with big-
brother disdain with Maggie and Liz, polite and
somewhat cold with others, but with Cassandra he had
always been warm. Always, that was, until grown-up
feelings and problems had destroyed their friendship.

Daniel had once been Cassandra's friend in the way that Liz and Maggie were still her friends. With him she had shared a simple loyalty, an uncomplicated affection. Until sex had come between them in the very same way it was threatening his offer of friendship right now. *And once again, it's all my fault,* Cassandra decided glumly.

Determined to put things right for once and for all, she straightened her shoulders. "You know, you're right, Daniel. Everything that's happened today comes from the past."

"Absolutely," he agreed.

Cassandra wondered if it was her overactive imagination or a trick of the light that made him look the tiniest bit disappointed. It's the light, she told herself firmly as she continued, "What I think I should do is go. And then tomorrow or the day after or whenever we see each other again, we can just pretend what happened today was one of those...uh...time warps or whatever."

Daniel laughed a little at that. "You know something, only you could make that seem reasonable."

"Great, then that's the plan, right?" Strangely reluctant to leave, Cassandra nevertheless went across the room to get her jacket and purse.

"Wait a minute," Daniel said, making her turn back to face him. "Why not stay?" *Dear Lord, here I go again,* he thought, *issuing stupid invitations. Why can't I just let her go?*

"You want me to stay?" she murmured.

Too much, he said silently, even as his lips formed the words, "Why not?"

Tempted despite her best judgment, Cassandra searched for a convenient excuse. "Oh...uh...I forgot that my parents are probably holding dinner for me."

He looked so skeptical that she started scrambling for another reason to leave. She couldn't have Daniel thinking she was afraid to be alone with him, even though she was. "I meant to say it's Maggie who's waiting for me."

Let her go, Daniel repeated silently, but instead he said, "So Maggie and Don decided not to go to Atlanta this weekend?"

"Did I say Maggie? I meant Li—" Cassandra stopped and lifted her chin. "Oh, for God's sake, Daniel, you know I don't have any plans." Courage, she told herself, courage was what she needed, and it was best developed under a test of fire. She'd be better off if she stayed for a pleasant, *friendly* evening with Daniel. It could set the stage for a new relationship with him, the friendship she'd been determined to have before the old chemistry had started working between them. Yes, she could be his friend.

"I'll stay," she announced, holding up her empty wineglass. "How about some more of this?"

Her ebony eyes were sparkling, her face was glowing against her dark hair, her curves were displayed to best advantage in her clinging knit sundress. She presented a picture that would elicit a reaction from most men, especially from a man who already knew the sweetly intoxicating taste of her lips.

How, Daniel wondered, *how am I going to make it through this evening without kissing her again?*

To his immense relief, Cassandra seemed determined to talk her way through whatever awkward moments they encountered. Soon he was almost able to relax. There was no danger of running out of things to talk about, since he and Cassandra hadn't really talked in years. Maggie had kept them each apprised of the major events in the other's life, but there were plenty of gaps to be filled in.

In Daniel's narrow black-and-white kitchen, Cassandra talked nonstop about the school while the steaks were placed in a marinade and potatoes were popped into the microwave. Then she raided his refrigerator and cabinets for salad ingredients. They both chopped vegetables while she regaled him with stories about her struggles in the world of entertainment.

Her first two years in New York had included the usual schedule of acting, voice and dance classes, auditions, callbacks and disappointments. Then she had become part of a cabaret act that toured South America, where, as their manager had assured them, they were all going to become stars.

Knife poised over a tomato, Daniel stared at her. "In South America?"

"It sounded good at the time," Cassandra defended. "You know, Rio de Janeiro, sun, sand, ritzy hotels. It was great until this Brazilian gangster decided he wanted me as his bride."

"A gangster?" Daniel echoed. Drugs. Machine guns. Blood in the streets. The vision that rose to mind had the makings of a made-for-TV movie. "You're kidding, aren't you?"

Blithely Cassandra dumped a can of artichoke hearts into a colander to drain. "Actually, Enrico wasn't nearly as bad as the modeling agent in Paris."

"I didn't know you modeled in Paris."

"I didn't," she retorted. "*Monsieur* Pierre and I couldn't come to terms."

"Terms?"

She wrinkled her nose and dropped her voice. "Pierre had weird ways of getting his kicks, and he definitely had no qualms about mixing business with what *he* called pleasure." Her grin faded to a frown as she admonished, "Daniel, you're pulverizing that poor tomato. Give it to me and go sit down."

While Daniel tried not to think about what could have happened to Cassandra in Paris, she took over the salad preparation. He perched on a stool at the bar that separated the kitchen from the dining room, surprised by how at-home Cassandra looked in the kitchen. He had learned to cook in self-defense against his mother's culinary disasters, and there were times when he could admit to enjoying the task. But he'd never known Cassandra to take to food preparation with the enthusiasm she showed now.

"Where did you learn to do this?" he asked as she neatly quartered another tomato.

"Daniel, it's just a salad, not a soufflé."

"Do you do soufflés?"

"I've attempted a few."

Getting up to retrieve another beer from the refrigerator, he laughed.

"You sound doubtful."

He leaned against the cabinet and laughed again. "Remember, I was at my grandparents' every Christmas when you brought over that fudge you used to make. It weighed a ton and had the consistency of uncrushed gravel."

"You mean you didn't really like my fudge?"

"After you left, my grandmother's housekeeper always threw it in the garbage. She stopped putting it into the disposal after it broke a blade."

Cassandra sniffed. "Well, it's nice to know my efforts were so appreciated."

"Oh, they were appreciated, just not eaten."

"Times have changed," she said stiffly. "I'm now a quite passable cook. I had to learn."

"And why is that?"

"A simple matter of survival."

"Uh-huh." Daniel hadn't really intended to sound so skeptical, but it was hard for him to imagine that Cassandra had ever really needed to cook. Not with all her money.

She paused in the act of adding the tomatoes to the salad. "How do you think I ate in New York and Brazil and Paris and everywhere else? People do have to eat, you know, even in exotic ports of call."

"Didn't Pierre and Enrico and God knows who else take you out?"

He made it sound as if she'd dated half the population of the cities in question. That made Cassandra bristle. "For your information, most of the men I went out with were struggling actors or singers or dancers just like me."

"Oh, so you paid for dinner?"

"Sometimes," she said defensively. "And sometimes I boiled hot dogs and opened a can of chili."

"Yeah, your grandfather's trust fund could probably keep you in lots of franks and beans," Daniel taunted, eyes narrowing as he sipped his beer again.

Anger started a slow burn in the pit of Cassandra's stomach. "This is the last time I'm going to tell you this, Daniel, so I hope you'll listen. I'm not the same as I was when I was eighteen. A lot has happened between then and now, and I have changed."

Fuming, she threw the artichokes into the salad bowl and continued, "I'm the first to admit that I had a lot more money than most people in my situation. And I also admit that managing my money wasn't and isn't my strongest point. I have been known to be extravagant and impetuous from time to time."

"I know," he put in. "Remember, I've seen that warehouse you bought."

She glared at him. "But contrary to what you think, I've not spent the last dozen or so years eating at the best restaurants, sipping fine wines and mingling with the jet set." As if to emphasize her point, she seized a wooden salad fork and plunged it into the bowl, tossing vegetables with a vengeance. "Maybe I didn't suffer in an artist's garret, but I didn't have a maid to bring a breakfast tray and copy of *Variety* to my room each morning, either. I was out there, pounding the pavement like millions of other hardworking, talented people. And I did manage to learn how to toss myself a salad and heat up a can of soup."

Daniel was silent when she finished the speech. That made her even angrier. "You know, you really have no room to criticize me because I inherited some money. Your grandparents surely didn't leave you a pauper."

"Why would you say that?" he returned, intently studying the floor, his dark spiky lashes shielding the expression in his eyes from her view.

"Well," she faltered, "they just couldn't have."

He looked up, and the coolness of his gaze passed over Cassandra like a winter's breeze. "And what makes you think my grandfather would leave anything to the offspring of the Irish scum who ruined his precious daughter?''

"You mean he left you nothing?" Cassandra whispered, flabbergasted.

"I don't know why you're so surprised. You know how he felt about my mother and Maggie and me."

"But I thought he mellowed out. He was paying for your college, wasn't he? I thought—"

"If you'll remember, it was my junior year that Grandfather died. Mother, Maggie and I weren't mentioned in his will. The house and everything else was divided up among my uncles. To Uncle Bob's credit, he did pay the rest of my college, and he offered to do more, but I told him to forget it."

"But that's horrible—"

"I didn't need his charity," Daniel snapped.

"I mean your grandfather was horrible. I know he hated your father, but to treat you and Maggie like that . . ." Cassandra swallowed hard. How could anyone be so cruel? "He wouldn't have done it if your grandmother had been alive. She wouldn't have let him."

"But she was gone, too." Though a flicker of pain crossed his face, Daniel shrugged. "Anyway, I think I've done just fine without the old man's money. It was Maggie I was really sorry for. She had a hard time after the baby died and Barry left her."

"I could have helped," Cassandra murmured. "Why didn't Maggie say something? She never told me she needed money."

Daniel shook his head. "Get serious, will you? We may have been broke, but Maggie and I had our pride. Maybe we inherited that from one of Dad's ancestors. The trait must skip generations."

"But Maggie could have told me," Cassandra insisted.

"You were in New York, a lifetime away."

Cassandra swallowed hard. Was it his tone of voice or her own guilt that made his statement sound so accusatory. She hadn't come home for his mother's funeral, much less his grandfather's. At that point, she hadn't even been speaking to Daniel on her few fleeting visits.

"Eugenia helped," Daniel said, breaking into her thoughts. He smiled a little. "That woman has a way of taking care of things before you even know what she's about."

Cassandra lifted an eyebrow. "You think you're telling me something I don't know?"

"I guess not."

For a moment they gazed at each other in amusement, then Cassandra sobered again. "I'm sorry for the way things worked out with your grandfather, Daniel. He was a foolish old man."

"I won't argue on that point," he replied, straightening away from the cabinets. "But I've done okay, even without his money. I expect to do even better. All on my own. I found out early you can't count on anyone but yourself."

The harshness of his voice echoed around the room, and Cassandra's sense of guilt returned with a vengeance. No doubt she had helped Daniel develop the attitude, as if he'd needed any help after the way his parents had treated him. She wanted to argue with his cold and bitter attitude, but he turned away before she could find the right words.

"Daniel—"

"I'm going out to the patio," he said, cutting her off. "I think it's time to put these on." He lifted the plate of marinating filets from the counter and started to leave.

Though her thoughts were still churning over what he had told her, Cassandra automatically opened a cabinet to search for some dinner plates. The sound of Daniel speaking her name made her turn.

He stood beside the bar, looking uncomfortable. "I'm sorry for some of the things I've said and for the way I've acted yesterday and today."

"Sorry?"

"For judging you on the basis of how you used to be," he explained, paraphrasing one of her earlier accusations. "Maybe I was wrong. Maybe people really do change." With that, he turned and walked through the dining room to the patio beyond.

His last words chased around and around in Cassandra's head while she set the table for dinner. *Maybe people change.* How true was that? How different were she and Daniel now from who they'd been twelve years ago? Down deep, where it really mattered, they might not have changed at all.

The thought momentarily terrified her. She'd spent months trying to convince everyone that she was different, that she was no longer content to roll through life without a definite purpose. She had to have changed. Two months from now she was going to be right here running the school. She was going to stick with something until it worked. She wouldn't get bored or discouraged. She'd show everyone she could do it. Everyone, including herself. Including Daniel.

That vow, however, only seemed to prove her earlier fear. By God, there were some things that hadn't changed at all. For winning Daniel's approval was what she had always tried to do. If she examined her motives honestly, she might even discover he was part of the reason she had come home.

"Oh, Lord, no," Cassandra whispered as she gripped the cushioned back of a dining room chair for support.

Through the glass doors leading to the patio, she could see Daniel. From this distance, in the dim light, with his tie discarded and sleeves rolled up, he looked little older than he'd been twelve years ago. The years hadn't really changed his just-short-of handsome features, and as it had been so often in the past, his expression was pensive, the set of his mouth vaguely unhappy. Once upon a time she could have kissed that unhappiness away. No matter how bad it got—when his mother was drunk and his father was off on some binge of his own, Cassandra had always been able to lift Daniel up, the same as he could keep her rooted in reality.

What would have happened if they had stayed together?

That was the question Cassandra had never allowed herself to get lost in. But now it beckoned like a path at the edge of a maze. *What if she explored that path?*

Taken as always by the thought of a new challenge, Cassandra forgot everything she had said and promised about just being Daniel's friend. For who wanted plain white bread when they could have it with peanut butter and jelly? Certainly not Cassandra. At last she would explore those feelings she had only packed away but never discarded.

What if? Those had to be the most intriguing two words in the English language. Especially when she applied them to a man she had never quite been able to forget.

She'd have to be subtle, of course, because Daniel really thought he could resist her. He'd probably fight her every step of the way. But she would win.

Eugenia was right all along, Cassandra thought, watching Daniel as he lifted the steaks from the grill. Quickly she reached for the dimmer switch on the dining-room light. Not too dark, but not too bright, either. There was no time like the present to put her plan in motion.

The mood was friendly as they sat down to dinner, but Daniel couldn't help eyeing Cassandra with suspicion. She reminded him of nothing so much as a cat with a bowl of cream...or with a cornered mouse. That idea made him frown. Distrustfully he glanced across the table at her smile.

She lifted her glass of wine. "A toast, Daniel?"

"Sure," he replied, his eyes steady on hers. "To old friends."

"Oh, yes," she replied, touching her glass to his. "To friendship."

For the life of him, Daniel couldn't see what it was about that toast that made her laugh so hard.

Five

The house where Eugenia lived was in a section of Nashville where old money was more prevalent than new, where bankers still outnumbered country music stars. Home to five generations of her family, the house was built of mellowed brick and stone, half covered by ivy and surrounded by a broad expanse of landscaped lawn. On this late June Sunday, it seemed to Daniel that every blade of grass in that yard was trimmed to the same height and that every flower in each well-placed bed and border was blooming. He paused halfway down the curving front sidewalk for a moment of silent appreciation.

As though she could read his thoughts, Cassandra slipped her hand into the crook of his elbow. "It looks perfect today, doesn't it?"

Daniel nodded, thinking the word perfection could also be applied to Cassandra. Against her sunshine-yellow dress, her hair looked as black as midnight, and her dark eyes were sparkling. She was as vibrant as the summer day itself. He almost told her how beautiful she was but then thought better of it. Talk like that was hardly the right sort for their new, chummy relationship.

Chummy. It was a ridiculous description. But incredibly, it was appropriate. In the two weeks since Cassandra had had dinner at his place, they had shared other meals, seen another movie and, just last night, attended a concert at the school. And here they were—together again. If he wasn't so dead set on showing her she didn't affect him at all, he could avoid her. As it was, however, he never seemed to have a good excuse not to see her. So they spent plenty of time in each other's company. It was all very nice and friendly. And all very torturous for Daniel.

He would begin each of their encounters with the best of intentions, but inevitably Cassandra would smile at him or touch his hand and an ache would start deep in his gut. Why, he wondered as he continued to gaze at her, why had he put himself in this situation?

That question and its elusive answer had given him several headaches in the past few weeks, and that wasn't how he wanted to spend this beautiful summer afternoon. So instead Daniel concentrated on the scene before him.

Cassandra was still studying the house. "Isn't it funny how we think of this as Eugenia's house, even though it isn't? I mean, it really belongs to Liz's mother and father."

"And someday it will be Liz and Nathan's."

"I bet everyone will still think of it as Eugenia's, even then."

"Speaking of Eugenia..." Daniel glanced at his watch. "I imagine she's pouring tea right about now."

"Oh, blast it, are we late?" Cassandra asked as she slipped her hand from his arm and continued toward the house. "I honestly tried to be on time, Daniel, I really did."

"Since when do you worry about being late?"

Without bothering to ring the doorbell of what had always been her second home, Cassandra opened the front door and grinned over her shoulder at him. "It's not me I'm worried about. I just don't want to tarnish your sterling image."

"Let me worry about my own image."

"Aye-aye, sir." She gave him a smart but playful salute, then slipped into a Mae West accent. "Just remember, big boy, you could get a reputation hangin' round with me."

Laughing at her antics, Daniel took hold of her elbow as they crossed the wide foyer. They were still laughing and completely absorbed in each other when they paused in the front parlor's doorway.

The silence was what finally drew Daniel's attention. Glancing up, he found five people, immobile as figures in a wax museum, their eyes riveted on him and Cassandra. His gaze slid from face to face. His sister, Maggie, was smiling in a knowing sort of way while her date looked around in bewilderment. Liz, discreet soul that she was, was trying not to show her surprise. Her husband, Nathan, had a touch of sympathy in his face. Eugenia appeared simply delighted, and it was her expression that made Daniel draw away from Cassandra.

She, however, was not one to let a dramatic moment pass without milking it for all it was worth. "For

Pete's sake," she declared in brash Brooklynese. "You all look as if you came for the reading of the will. Who died, anyways?"

Like floodwater over a dam, laughter covered the remaining awkwardness. Yet Daniel cursed himself silently for not realizing how it would feel to walk into this room with Cassandra on his arm. Three of the people here knew how it had been between them all those years ago. Each of them had tried at one time or another to play matchmaker. He felt as if every movement he made was being scrutinized, dissected and filed away for future reference. Only his sister's date and Liz's husband had no interest in *Daniel-and-Cassandra-and-what-they-were-doing-together*, so he started toward the men.

But of course it was Eugenia who put a stop to his retreat. "Daniel," she said, patting the cushion beside hers on the couch. "You must sit down and tell me everything that's been happening. Have you been helping Cassandra decide how to spend Herbert's money on her school?"

It was more an order than a request. Daniel soon found himself seated beside her, drinking an unwanted cup of tea and wishing with every passing moment that he had put a little thought into what this afternoon tea party would entail.

From across the room, Cassandra studied Daniel's discomfited expression with amusement. Beside her, Liz's laughter was soft.

"Well, well, well, Cassandra dear," Liz murmured. "No wonder I haven't seen much of you in the last couple of weeks. It looks as if you've been busy."

Cassandra sipped her tea, nonchalantly pretending to misunderstand. "Oh, I've been very busy. The school, you know."

"That's not what I meant."

"But what else could you mean, Liz dear?"

Before Liz could reply, Maggie joined them, her brown eyes dancing with merriment. She got right to the point. "Cassandra, what are you and Daniel up to?"

Cassandra feigned an intense interest in the pattern of flowers on her china teacup while she murmured, "Whatever do you mean?"

"Don't give me the innocent act," Maggie retorted, then glanced at Daniel and lowered her voice. "You've been seeing an awful lot of him."

"It's business."

Liz rolled her eyes. "That's utter nonsense."

"And that's putting it nicely," Maggie added.

Cassandra set her teacup down in its saucer. "Good heavens, can't two old friends spend some time together without everyone getting upset?"

"Old friends?" Liz echoed. "That's not exactly the description I'd use for you and Daniel."

"Besides," Maggie added. "No one's upset. Personally, I hope you turn my brother's neat little world topsy-turvy." With a wink and a twirl of her full pink cotton skirt, she headed across the room to join her date, who was in deep discussion with Liz's husband.

"I wish she'd take her own advice," Liz muttered. "That man of hers doesn't know the meaning of topsy-turvy, unless of course you're referring to the crash of '29."

Nodding in agreement, Cassandra watched Maggie slip her arm through her date's. "Daniel says he can't understand why we don't like Don."

"Well, that's what I might expect from Daniel," Liz replied. "For such a smart man, there are times when he can be pretty dense."

Cassandra grinned. "No argument on that point from me."

Liz hesitated for a moment, and her blue eyes grew thoughtful. "He doesn't like to be trifled with, either," she said softly. "You should know that better than anyone."

The warning in her words was obvious to Cassandra, even though it was unnecessary. For she knew Daniel wasn't someone with whom she could play games. She also knew this wasn't a game. She was searching for the answer to an old and troubling question. No matter how it turned out between herself and Daniel, they'd both be better off if they explored the possibilities of what had once been tossed aside so carelessly.

When Cassandra made no reply to her observation, Liz sighed and frowned slightly. But she said nothing else about Daniel. Instead, she nodded once more to the group across the room. "I think I'd better rescue Nathan. He looks dazed, sort of like he did the time Don gave him a point-by-point description of the day's trading on the Japanese stock market."

Cassandra chuckled as she watched Liz take over the conversation with the ease of the polished trial attorney that she was. Don's boring monologue didn't stand a chance against her. A quick glance at the room's other occupants showed that Eugenia was still talking with Daniel, so Cassandra turned to the side table, which held a tempting spread of food.

Afternoon tea was a habit Eugenia had acquired after a long acquaintance with an English journalist who had lived in Paris. He had been one of Eugenia's many fiancés. She had told the girls fascinating tales about him, during the weekly tea parties she had thrown when they were younger. She talked about him still, every chance she got. Cassandra thought the man had been Eugenia's one great love. To honor his memory, her Sunday tea was always served in the traditional British style, and that meant enough food to qualify it as a full meal. Today was no exception, and Cassandra was busy loading a plate when a voice spoke low beside her.

"I hear you are up to some mischief, *chérie*."

Cassandra turned to meet a pair of sparkling eyes. "Jeannette," she said in delight, grinning at the plump gray-haired Frenchwoman who had been Eugenia's cook, maid and companion for over thirty years. Cassandra gave her a little hug. "Now, Jeannette, why would you ever think I'd be into any mischief?" she asked.

Pausing in her unnecessary replenishment of a tray of cakes, Jeannette lifted an eyebrow. "I'm an old woman, and I know enough about life to know some things do not change. And you've been in trouble more than out since I came to this house."

"Me? Trouble?"

Jeannette slanted a sideways glance at Daniel, who was still caught in Eugenia's clutches. "Maybe the trouble is for someone else?"

"And is that bad?"

Dimples appeared in the woman's rounded cheeks. "I say maybe he needs a little trouble, no?"

"My feelings exactly."

Jeannette's laughter lingered even after she left the room. Amused, Cassandra turned back to the room and found herself looking straight into Daniel's eyes, an action that gave her a curiously breathless sensation. She had felt this way many times in the past couple of weeks. Had it been like this all those years ago? No, it was more intense now, perhaps because she kept comparing the feeling to the times she had stood center stage while a casting director sat in the darkened seats at the back of a theater. Nerves and adrenaline and excitement were jumbled inside her.

Those familiar emotions collided as Cassandra smiled at Daniel. She hoped for a response, but he looked away. How silly, she thought.

No matter how he tried to pretend, she knew he was weakening under her subtle, friendly plan of attack. Cassandra nibbled at a cream-cheese-and-cucumber sandwich, mentally reviewing the past two weeks. Yes, there had been many times when he had betrayed his true feelings. A darkening of his eyes when she laughed up at him. A stiffening of his muscles when her strategically placed but most casual touch lingered a moment longer than necessary. If only he would give in and put his arms around her again. To be in his arms—that was all she needed.

All? Cassandra's gaze lingered for a moment on Daniel's strong broad hands...on the tanned neck revealed by the open collar of his white shirt...on the firm set of his decidedly masculine mouth. No, her needs wouldn't stop when she was in his arms. That's when they'd begin.

She took a deep breath, surprised by the erotic turn her thoughts had taken. Not that they were new thoughts where Daniel was concerned. There had been an earlier time when she had burned for his touch. The heat was just stronger now. It was no longer the untutored yearning of a teenager. She wanted Daniel. Standing here in a room full of people where he wouldn't even look at her, she wanted him with a fierceness that pulsed all the way to the deepest, most secret part of her.

Surely everyone can tell, Cassandra thought, glancing down at her plate of food in embarrassment. Surely everything she felt was showing on her face. She let out a breath, tried to compose herself and looked at Daniel again. He had remained on the couch while Eugenia had joined the others to recount some outlandish tale about her Englishman. The voices and laughter faded to the background as Cassandra stared into Daniel's brown eyes. This time it was his gaze that trapped hers, holding her as surely as his strong male body might press her backward into the giving softness of a bed.

Not the best comparison to be thinking of right now, she berated herself.

Yet she allowed the image to linger. She even embellished it, imagining the feel of Daniel's hands on her breasts. Lifting. Stroking. Teasing. And all the while his eyes would be on hers, promising more delights to come.

Lost in the fantasy, Cassandra felt her nipples tighten in eager anticipation, and the sensation returned her to reality. She and Daniel weren't alone. They weren't even touching. Yet she continued to look at Daniel, convinced he was every bit as aroused as she. How could he know what she was thinking? How had he always known?

With an effort, Cassandra managed to break free of the spell that bound her to Daniel. Her hands were shaking as she turned back to the tea table, and she set her plate down with a loud clatter.

"Anything wrong?" Eugenia called from across the room.

Cassandra wouldn't, couldn't turn around. Not while Daniel was still sitting there watching her. "Just clumsy old me," she returned with what she hoped would pass for unconcern. Then she murmured, "Excuse me," and escaped from the room.

Her exit, hasty though it was, caused barely a ripple of interest in the others. Daniel continued to hold his breath and prayed no one would try to draw him into the conversation. Slowly he unclenched his fists. Now if only the tightness that gripped the rest of his body would leave as easily. It was a poor state of affairs when a grown man found himself reacting like a teenager experiencing his first taste of passion.

But Cassandra had been his first taste of passion.

And no one else had ever matched those sweet imaginings.

It's just the lure of the unknown, Daniel reassured himself. Hoping the others would continue to ignore him, he got to his feet and crossed to the window. Yes, it was the mystery that had him daydreaming in public about Cassandra. And it was nonsense to think she might be sharing those same fantasies.

But there had been something in her glance. Something full of hot promise. It reminded him of how she had looked the first time they had done more than kiss.

That memory was burning so brightly, Daniel didn't realize his sister had joined him, until her voice penetrated his introspection.

"Is everything all right?" Maggie asked.

Nodding automatically, Daniel glanced down at his pretty blond sister. For a moment, he was tempted to tell her the truth, that nothing was okay. What would Maggie say if he told her he had been thinking about taking Cassandra to bed, about finally burning off the foolish young passion he'd once had for his sister's best friend?

The temptation passed as quickly as it took Daniel to consider it. Even if Maggie and Cassandra weren't such good friends, he could never share such an intimate confidence with his sister. Perhaps their distance wasn't an unusual occurrence between brothers and sisters, but they'd had every reason to become close over the years. In the storm that had been their family, each could have used the other as an anchor.

Daniel had to admit that Maggie had tried to reach out to him. Just as he had held her away. Calling her at one in the morning to ask if she really thought Cassandra was capable of running a school was perhaps the most spur-of-the-moment conversation he had initiated with her in the past five years. Maggie hadn't acted as if there were anything unusual about him calling at that time of night, although she must have thought it extremely odd. Taking things in stride was just the way she operated.

She smiled now and lightly touched the lapel of his navy sport jacket. That was Maggie for you, always touching, pampering, smoothing things over. "I'm glad you came today," she said simply before going back to the others.

Watching her, Daniel sighed again. Where did she get that serenity of hers? That calmness had always been a part of her. He had once resented it, for he hadn't thought it fair that she could take injustices so easily, not when they filled him with bitterness and anger. Only twice had he seen Maggie come unglued. There was that terrible night when her baby had died. And an earlier night, the time she had taken the punishment their mother had intended for him.

How alien, how ugly that memory seemed as Daniel stood in this beautiful room and stared at the bright, perfect day outside. He shut his eyes, blocking the sunshine, wishing he could block the pain of the past. It came, however, with relentless clarity, leaving the sour taste of hatred in his mouth.

Something had frozen inside him the night his mother had hit Maggie. After that only Cassandra had been able to reach past the ice. Then she had hurt him, betrayed him, and no one else had ever come as close.

With that cold thought in mind, Daniel turned to watch Cassandra come back to the room. He tried his best to study her with cool detachment. But as always there was something about her smile. Something warm and exciting and a little bit reckless. Dammit, she made him care. More now than ever.

"I don't know about you guys," she announced to the room. "But I think we should keep this party going on into the evening."

Eugenia, who had seated herself with regal grace on the sofa, smiled. "Looking for something more exciting than tea and crumpets, Cassandra?"

Cassandra perched on the arm of the sofa and gave her a hug. "You know I adore your tea parties, Eugenia."

"But?"

"But wouldn't you all rather go to an amusement park?"

She was greeted by a chorus of boos and hisses and groans. But with Cassandra doing the persuading, Daniel wasn't really surprised to find himself, a scant two hours later, seated beside her in the front seat of a roller coaster. Behind them were Liz and Nathan, and somewhere in the crowd of people jamming the Opryland theme park were Maggie and Don, who had begged off this ride. Only Eugenia had stayed home, protesting that throngs of tourists were the only people who could still intimidate her.

"She should have come," Cassandra insisted as their car rattled and squeaked its way up the first hill of the ride. "The doctor says her heart is as strong as a forty-year-old's. I think she might have liked this."

"I'm thirty-two, and I'm not sure I like it," Daniel muttered.

Cassandra grinned. "You're going to love it, Daniel, I promise."

"I seem to remember you saying that at other crucial moments of my life, and one of us always ended up with a cast or some stitches." The car came to a stop then, poised on the brink of a dizzying plunge.

Daniel glanced around him, noting the summer sun that hung like a giant orange ball on the horizon. The smell of hot buttered popcorn was so heavy he could taste it. The car moved and he gripped the steel bar in front of him. He felt the softness of Cassandra's hand as she laid it over his. He glanced at her. She blinked.

And they fell off the edge of the world.

Why don't I remember it being like this? Cassandra wondered as they hurtled downward and upward and twisted sideways. Earlier she had been aching for Daniel's touch in a room full of people. Now she was at an amusement park, on a roller coaster, for crying out loud, and all she knew was she was going to die if he didn't kiss her soon. And as soon as they kissed, she knew she was going to want so much more.

She had suggested they come here—to one of her favorite places in the world—because she wanted to get away from these feelings Daniel was arousing. Not that she didn't enjoy the feelings, not that they hadn't been her aim all along. But she hadn't counted on them leaving her so confused. Or on wanting him in this desperate sort of way.

Her feelings for him should be simple and neat, in the way that Daniel's life without her looked to be. The way Cassandra had imagined most normal people's lives to be. After all, if you didn't go off chasing dreams on stages all over the world, your life was supposed to be calm and easy. Wasn't it? Well, she was through chasing dreams. So why was what was happening between her and Daniel as scary as a fast ride on a narrow, twisting track?

Cassandra still had no answer for that when the roller coaster roared to a halt a few minutes later. And she felt as giddy as ever when she looked at Daniel. All she knew was that she had been wrong earlier. It would matter how it turned out between them. If it didn't work, her heart was going to be broken again.

After agreeing to meet the other two couples later, they wandered through the park. The day had faded with a spectacular sunset. The tourists of Eugenia's worst fears were thronging the flower-edged paths, and lights were bathing everything in the peculiar neon glow of a carnival. Every corner revealed another kind of music, another ice-cream stand, another fast and furious ride.

Cassandra loved these sights and sounds. But it was Daniel who fascinated her tonight. The way he walked. The way his light brown hair ruffled in the evening breeze. Especially the way he smiled when he caught her looking at him.

"You'd better watch it," she murmured as they paused beside a cotton candy cart. "That reputation of yours we talked about earlier will be shot all to hell if you keep looking so happy."

It occurred to Daniel that he was happy. In a disconcerting, unexpectedly sloppy sort of way, too. "I guess I'm into taking chances tonight," he said. "It'll be business as usual tomorrow, I'm sure."

"I hope not." The words came out so fast even Cassandra looked startled.

"Why is that?"

Her gaze met his and held. Steady. Serious. "Because I want you to be happy," she answered without a trace of guile.

He caught her hand in his, not in the simple way that friends touch, but in the way a man holds a woman's hand when he can't stand not to touch her. In the same way, he traced a finger over the strong, pure line of her jaw. And then he kissed her, the lightest, sweetest kiss possible. But even at that, it sizzled.

"Cassandra," Daniel murmured, pulling away. "Please let's not..." He paused. He'd been about to say they shouldn't hurt each other. But that wasn't what he wanted to say. That said far too much. "Please let's not push it..." he finally murmured.

Her eyes widened, and he could see she again spoke from her heart. "Daniel, I don't even know what I'm pushing for."

He laughed then, softly, and drew his hand through the curling tendrils of her hair. That was an old gesture, left over from their past. Daniel could see by Cassandra's expression that she was remembering it, the same as he, and for some reason he wanted tonight to belong to the here and now.

"Let's go ride the roller coaster again," he said, drawing her back into the flow of tourists.

"So you've decided you like a thrill now and then, huh?"

He squeezed her hand. "I had forgotten how much fun thrills can be."

Cassandra knew he was talking about them, not a silly amusement park ride, and happiness spread through her. This time, when their car had stopped just before the first slide, she kissed him.

And as expected, her stomach was doing flip-flops before they even started over the edge.

What a ride, she thought, what a crazy, glorious ride this might turn out to be.

Exhilaration carried Cassandra through the next few weeks. With Daniel by her side, she floated through a Fourth of July when the fireworks over Nashville had nothing on the ones going off inside of her. The usual summer heat wave was tame compared to what brewed between them. Daniel and Cassandra were absorbed in each other, and neither of them bothered to hide their deepening involvement.

Her parents were astounded yet curiously pleased. Claire and William Martin had always regarded the grandson of their next-door neighbors as a good match for their flighty, dream-chasing daughter, despite the problems in his family when he was younger. They were actually speaking to Cassandra by the time they left for their annual two months in the mountains.

Liz and Maggie regarded Cassandra and Daniel with a cautious optimism. Eugenia, who seemed to be spending an inordinate amount of time with a certain Herbert Black, sent Cassandra a bouquet of her favorite red roses. The card read, "Bravo. Now aren't you glad I meddled?" To that, Cassandra could only say a big, fat yes.

It wasn't that there was anything too deep about the changes in her relationship with Daniel. He was still a cautious man. Cassandra knew that, and she didn't expect him to move hastily into anything. In the cool, logical moments when they were apart, she accepted that without qualm. When he looked at her, touched her, kissed her, oh, but then it was a different matter entirely. Then she was impatient, ready for the next step.

But just as he had asked, she didn't push. Cassandra was proud of that. For the first time in her life, she was doing the right things, in the accepted ways. She and Daniel were getting to know each other again. That was the most important thing now.

They talked. About old times. About what had happened to each of them in the ensuing years. About everyday matters and global problems. Cassandra never ran out of things to say to Daniel. In turn, she was fascinated by everything he had to tell her. There was only one topic they left untouched, and that was what had happened between them years ago. Cassandra decided that was probably a wise decision. They couldn't change yesterday, but tomorrow was wide open.

Her school was thriving right along with her personal life. At the end of a long day, she was filled with immense satisfaction. She continued to love working with the kids. On the last weekend of the month, the high-school group would present their second play of the summer, and Cassandra had invited local dignitaries, members of the media and potential backers to a special gala premiere. She and the cast and crew were working extra hard to make it an impressive event, but she didn't mind the long hours. Cassandra thought she could do this forever. And forever wasn't a concept she had bothered with much in the past.

Daniel spent much of his free time at the school with her. He worried about her being there alone when she locked up after play practice or late rehearsal. She told him he was being silly and overprotective. After all, she had traveled the globe; she could take care of herself. But secretly his concern was welcome. It showed he cared.

As absorbed as she was in what she was doing, Cassandra could always tell when Daniel was there. Something, a sixth sense perhaps, alerted her, and she would look up and find him at the door of her office or seated quietly in the back of the theater. His presence made her feel warm and needed. Increasingly he was shadowed by a new friend.

Matt Barker had attached himself to Daniel. Maybe it was because the troubled boy so desperately needed a father figure. Whatever the reason, he liked Daniel.

The feeling was mutual. Daniel seemed to see in the boy something of himself at that age. As Daniel had been, Matt was a mass of confused and angry emotions. Something—Daniel's grandmother or Cassandra, for a time—had kept those feelings from exploding where Daniel was concerned. He and Cassandra worried that Matt wouldn't be so lucky. The world was a pretty frightening place for a kid who thought no one loved him.

Daniel drove toward the school on a hot night in late July. His Thursday evening racquetball game had run longer than expected. He had enjoyed the exercise, but the thought of Cassandra alone at the school was now making him uneasy. There had been a string of rapes in Nashville recently. None of them had been in the school's community, but a person couldn't be too safe. And Cassandra could be so careless sometimes. Without him, she . . .

His strong protective urge made Daniel pause. He pulled to a stop in front of the school and sat unmoving for a moment, staring up at the brightly lit square that was Cassandra's office window. Everything was happening so fast between them.

"Fast?" Daniel murmured, chuckling as he opened the car door and stepped out into the muggy night. What was between him and Cassandra had been in the making their entire lives. Most people wouldn't find that too fast.

Still laughing, he tried the front door and found Cassandra had already locked it. Good girl, he thought, she had finally listened to his warnings. He went around to the side entrance and fumbled in his pocket for the key Cassandra had given him. He found it, but the old, rusting lock was stubborn. She needed to replace this door. It was probably the same age as the building, and without the deadbolt in place it provided little protection against a determined intruder.

The lock was still refusing to turn, and Daniel was growing irritated when he heard Cassandra's voice, raised in anger. Or was it fear? He paused, hair prickling on the back of his neck, until he heard a crash and the sound of breaking glass.

Then he said to hell with the key and kicked the door open.

Six

___

The vase filled with Eugenia's congratulatory roses joined a potted plant on the floor before Cassandra could make it around her desk to reach Matt's side. What had begun as disappointment and frustration had turned to anger, and for the first time she was frightened by the boy's violence. He just wouldn't listen to her.

"Matt, stop it," she yelled, trying yet again to make herself heard over his fury-filled oaths. "Matt, please, you've misunderstood—"

"Just hold it right there, Matt."

Turning, Cassandra found Daniel in the doorway, and relief swept through her. Until this moment, she hadn't realized how hard she'd been wishing he'd show up.

"Stop this nonsense," he said as he started toward Matt. "You know this kind of behavior doesn't prove anything. It doesn't get you anywhere."

The plant Matt had been holding crashed to the floor. The sound seemed to bring the boy to his senses. He looked up at Daniel and Cassandra, tears streaming from his blue eyes. But instead of the flush of anger, his face was pale, his freckles standing out like rust stains on ivory. Cassandra couldn't bear the pain in his expression.

"Matt," she murmured, stepping toward him.

He responded by bolting past her and eluding Daniel's outstretched hand.

"Dammit," Daniel muttered as he started after him.

Cassandra followed on his heels, but they were only halfway down the stairs when a door at the rear of the building banged shut. Though it was probably a useless chase, they continued down the stairs and through the darkened first floor to the back.

Daniel pushed open the back door and stood in the alley behind the school, calling Matt's name. In answer, his voice bounced off the surrounding buildings. There was no sign of Matt.

"Let's just go inside," Cassandra said when it was clear the boy wasn't going to respond. "Matt's angry and upset, but I think he'll be okay."

"That's not the point," Daniel retorted. "We can't just let him get away with little stunts like this. I know the kid has problems, but that's no excuse for tearing the place up."

"I'll talk to him."

"Talk to him, hell." Daniel wheeled around and stalked back inside the house. "I'm calling the police."

He moved so fast it was difficult for Cassandra to keep up, but she caught him just as he was punching a number into the phone on her desk. "No," she said firmly, pressing the receiver button down.

Daniel stared at her in surprise. "Cassandra, he tried to destroy your office."

"You're exaggerating. It's only a couple of plants."

"And what if you had gotten in the way of one of them?"

Resolutely Cassandra fought the memory of how frightened Matt's outburst had left her. "He wouldn't hurt me."

"How do you know?" Daniel demanded.

Cassandra stood her ground, meeting his angry gaze with unwavering confidence. Swearing softly, he tossed the phone to the desktop. She hung it up.

With hands crammed into the pockets of tight blue tennis shorts, Daniel stalked away from her. The shorts emphasized the powerful muscles of his thighs, and his white polo shirt hugged his masculine torso. At any other time, Cassandra could have fully appreciated his appearance. But when he turned around, what caught her attention most were the white lines of fury on either side of his mouth. She watched him in silence, waiting for his outburst.

He stopped pacing, but his hands were still held tight in his pockets as he faced her. "You're making a mistake, Cassandra. The kid needs help."

"And we're giving it to him. Nora works with him every week. Things have been going well—"

"Oh, yeah, things are so good that he turned on you."

"I made him angry."

"And that's an excuse?" His hands came out of his pockets, closed on her shoulders and tightened, but he didn't shake her, even though Cassandra could tell he wanted to.

"There's not an adolescent in the world who doesn't get angry over silly things."

"Yeah, but is that going to be a good enough excuse when Matt gets mad someday and blows someone's head off?"

She shrugged away from him, refusing to dwell on that possibility. "We're trying to help Matt avoid that kind of trouble."

His voice deepened, grew rough with emotion. "You can't do it on your own, Cassandra, and obviously Nora isn't getting through to him."

"He just got angry—"

"Just angry?" Pointedly Daniel studied the broken glass, ruined plants and potting soil that littered the floor near her desk. "If this is just angry, I'd hate to see him when he gets really upset."

"Daniel, you've spent time with Matt, and you know this was just an attempt to get attention."

"Yeah, I know that. I also know he's like a stick of dynamite, just waiting for something to light his fuse."

How true, Cassandra thought, at last allowing herself to relive those terrifying seconds when Matt's anger had flown wildly, unexpectedly out of control. God, she had been so scared. What would have happened if Daniel hadn't shown up when he did?

His quiet voice broke into her thoughts. "What caused this, Cassandra?"

She swallowed, glanced at the mess on the floor and then away again. "It was his play," she said finally. "The one he wrote."

"Oh." Daniel knew the play because Matt had asked him to read it last week. It was a surprisingly mature work and showed genuine talent. But it was also a bleak tale about a streetwise prince who loses everything and everyone he cares about. The moral of the story was quite clearly drawn from personal experience.

Cassandra had told Daniel that after making some changes in the play's gloomy message, she planned to have the younger kids' drama class stage it. She had hoped the attention would encourage Matt to continue focusing his energies on constructive activities. By helping him revise the ending, she hoped to show Matt that life didn't always take everything away.

"He didn't want to change it," she murmured, rubbing her bare arms as if she were chilled. "He got so mad. I kept trying to tell him that it wasn't that I didn't like the play, but that I wanted to work with him on it, to make it better. But he wouldn't listen. And I'm not so sure I should have suggested changing the ending." She looked up at Daniel with discouraged eyes. "It's like all he heard and all he understood was that I didn't like it."

"And by not liking it, you were, in a sense, taking it away from him."

She nodded. "He got so angry with me."

"He needs help," Daniel said again. "More help than he's getting. Maybe if we called the authorities in on this—"

"He'd never forgive me."

Dan perched on the edge of the desk and frowned at her. "Matt's forgiveness shouldn't be the issue, Cassandra. Maybe if we turn this incident in, they'll investigate his home again. Maybe they'll find something."

"Like what?" she challenged. "He's got food and clothes and a place to live. In the eyes of the authorities, that will probably make him one of the lucky ones."

"But you said abuse was suspected."

She laughed bitterly. "And never proven. The only kind of abuse that gets attention is the kind that leaves marks on the body. Unfortunately, the mental kind leaves just as many scars."

"But—"

"Oh, Daniel, what would the police do if we called them?" she asked, her voice rising. "Would they throw Matt in some juvenile hall?"

"That might be better than his home."

"Sure. And then again, he might meet up with some real little criminals, and they could teach him some new tricks about violence and hatred." She faced him with hands on her hips, her eyes blazing. "No, thanks, Daniel. This is my call, and when Matt walks in my door tomorrow or the day after—"

"You think he will?"

"I know he will," she insisted. "And when he does I'll listen to him and try to help him, because I know for damn sure that this school, *my* school, is just about the best thing that ever came into that boy's life."

Daniel pushed away from the desk and caught her hands in his. "Cassandra, I just...oh, hell." He pulled her into his arms. "You just don't know how scared I was when I heard you yelling. I imagined—"

"The worst," she completed for him, tipping her head back to look into his eyes. "And maybe you had reason. I really was frightened when Matt started throwing things around.''

''I can't believe you actually admitted to a weakness.''

''Thanks for being my knight in shining armor.''

''You may not thank me when you see how I kicked the side door in.''

''Kicked it?'' she echoed. ''You're kidding?''

''I just don't want anything to happen to you.''

''It won't.''

''Promise.'' Daniel hadn't intended that word be so fierce, but it came out that way, and the emotion behind it shook him hard.

Cassandra lifted a hand to his cheek. ''Daniel—''

His mouth crushed her lips, muffling whatever she might have said. This was no gentle kiss. Daniel made her lips open for him, plunging his tongue deep into her mouth, as if by that possession he could obliterate the notion that something horrible could have happened to her tonight.

He couldn't lose Cassandra.

Not when he'd finally found her again.

His hands slipped to the rounded curves of her bottom, pulling her hard against him. Desire mixed with his fear, and the combination left him desperate. Desperate, because he wasn't sure if he was ready for what his feelings for Cassandra implied.

His body was ready. Every tense, singing muscle ached to know her softness. He'd felt this way for weeks—hell, years. God, how he wanted her.

If he took Cassandra now, right now, as he should have all those years ago, maybe he would finally be sure. Maybe, if they took a second chance, she'd be the one person who would never let him down. Car-ing for someone, loving them, was a risk. That, Daniel had always known. And he usually didn't gamble. Now it could be different. If only he could take that chance.

He drew away from her, searching her passion-clouded features for some reassurance. That she wanted him was apparent. Her eyes were slumberous, her mouth still moist from his kiss and eager for more.

Groaning, he took her lips again, and the familiar spicy-sweet scent of her closed around him. She tasted of promises. Tempted beyond any man's endurance, Daniel's hand moved to the full breast that ripened against the thin material of her summer blouse. The sensation was heaven. The sound she made, half sigh and half moan, was enough to cause the most saintly of men to sell their souls.

While his thumb traced over the nipple that pebbled so sweetly at his touch, her hands slipped under his shirt, up the dampening skin of his back. Her touch made him hard and heavy with need.

"Daniel," she whispered, nibbling at his lower lip. "I promised not to push, but…" The tip of her tongue glided around his mouth. "But, please, Daniel. I want you so much. I know it will be so good."

"More than good," he murmured before plundering her mouth once more with his. Making love with Cassandra would show her exactly how much he cared.

But how much was that?

That question whispered through Daniel like the first cold wind of winter. And the answer turned the fire of his ardor to ice. Once more he was caught. Once more he had invested everything on the chance that Cassandra loved him.

And, God in heaven, how that scared him.

He pulled away and held her at arm's length.

Her lashes swept up, and she studied him with eyes full of passion. But passion wasn't all he wanted.

"Daniel?" she whispered, a frown drawing her brows together. "Daniel, what's wrong?"

He tried to think of how to explain it to her. But how could he tell her his fears? She'd only smile at him, wash over his hesitation with honeyed talk and sweet promises. And then they'd make love and he'd never stand a chance of getting out with his heart intact.

So instead of telling her what was really on his mind, he said, "This isn't right."

"Not right? But—"

"It's just not . . . not the right time."

"But Daniel—"

"I'm sorry." He moved away, not daring to look at her again. "Before I leave I'll fix the door downstairs so that no one can get in."

"But you can't go now."

"I have to," he muttered. Then he left.

Cassandra swayed forward, intending to follow him. But instead, she ended up in one of the chairs that faced her desk. She was shaking, although she wasn't sure if the cause was lingering arousal or overwhelming hurt.

"What happened?" she asked the still, deserted office. One minute they were a step away from ecstasy, and the next he was looking at her as if she were a stranger. And why?

Groaning, she lay her head against the back of her chair. God, how she wanted him. In every way. Sexually. Emotionally. More than anything, she wanted him to love her again. She wanted to love him back.

Loving Daniel was all she had ever wanted.

Why couldn't he want the same thing?

That question sent her head into her hands. Inevitably her thoughts took her back to another summer night when she had smarted from the sting of Daniel O'Grady's rejection.

She had been eighteen. He, barely twenty. They had been dating for almost four years. And, incredibly as it seemed to her now, they had never made love. But with every date that summer, they came a little bit closer. How was it the guys had referred to it then? Oh, yes, first base. Second. Wavering toward third. Then over again. The game they played was sexual tease.

Daniel had kept his head, of course. When Cassandra had completely lost hers, he had preached caution and birth control and a thousand-and-one other unromantic ideas. Cassandra, the spoiled child who always got what she wanted, had felt rejected and angry. She and Daniel had argued and broken up.

But that was no excuse for what she had done next.

That memory sent a flush burning up Cassandra's neck. She pushed herself out of the chair, wishing she could push her shame so easily aside. After twelve years, she could still remember each of the dirty names Daniel had called her then.

And dammit, she still felt as if she deserved every one of them.

Hugging her arms to her chest, she crossed the room to the window behind her desk. Outside, the summer moon was shrouded in clouds. It was the same moon that had shone down on her twelve years ago, and she had the same question to ask it.

What was she going to do about Daniel?

Why did I come?

Daniel asked himself that question for perhaps the fiftieth time in two hours. He had spent over a week trying not to think of Cassandra. Yet here he was at the school, and for him she was the only person in the room.

She was sparkling tonight, obviously thrilled with the attendance at the premiere of the play performed by her high-school group. Daniel had been skeptical when she had decided to make this a formal by-invitation-only event. Yet it had worked. The theater had been packed with politicians, members of the media, educators and others who were curious to see how the school was working. The performance had earned a standing ovation, and almost everyone had remained for this postproduction reception. Judging by the comments Daniel had heard, the school was scoring very favorable reviews.

At the center of it all was Cassandra, sexy in a black strapless dress. Her hair was loose, curling over her shoulders. Ruby earrings dripped from her ears, matching the ruby ring that flashed on her hand. She didn't look like a teacher, but teaching skills weren't what she needed to charm the benefactors she had included on the guest list. He imagined she'd get some new contributions after tonight.

From the position he had taken near the doorway to the school's largest meeting room, Daniel watched her smile into the eyes of a likely prospect. The sight of that smile left his mouth dry, so he took a sip of his champagne. His mother's drinking problem had taught him that alcohol doesn't solve anything. He had vowed never to follow her escape route, but there were times when he understood the reality-dampening allure of the stuff. Wanting to escape was the wrong reason to drink, however, so he placed his half-empty glass on a nearby table. He'd be better off drinking the punch the kids from the school were being served.

"Quite an event, isn't it?"

The husky sound of Eugenia's voice startled him. For a moment he had forgotten everything but Cassandra and the man she was talking with.

Eugenia chuckled before he could make a reply. "Why don't you just go talk to her?" she suggested.

He pretended not to understand. "Talk to who?"

She wasn't fooled. "So it's that bad, is it?" She patted him on the arm while a twinkle lit her bright blue eyes. "Cassandra told me you two were on the outs."

"Did she?" Daniel studied the crowd, trying to appear unconcerned.

"She wouldn't tell me why, though." There was a long, expectant pause. "I guess you're not going to tell me, either."

"Probably not."

"None of my business, right?"

"You could put it that way."

Eugenia laughed. "I've always liked your directness, Daniel. It's one of your best qualities."

"And here I believed you just thought I was cute." Despite his best efforts to stop it, a smile twitched at Daniel's lips.

"There now," Eugenia said. "I knew I could get you to smile."

"You always do."

"I wish I could solve your other problem as easily." She nodded in Cassandra's direction.

Daniel shrugged. "Even you can't work miracles."

"No, but I can give you some advice."

"Now why am I not surprised at that?"

Eugenia's expression grew somber. "Things haven't always been easy for you, Daniel. I know that much—"

"Eugenia," he cut in. "I really don't want—"

"No, now listen to me," she insisted. "Because I'm only going to say this to you once." Her gaze shifted to Cassandra. "You need her. You've always needed her."

Daniel looked around, nodded to a couple of people he knew and prayed for someone to rescue him. But evasive tactics had never worked with Eugenia in the past, so there was no reason to think they would now. He looked her straight in the eye. "Needing Cassandra just isn't enough."

"Of course it isn't. You have to love her, too."

"And get hurt? Isn't that what love brings you?"

"Daniel, Daniel," Eugenia sighed. "Did it ever occur to you not to assume the worst?"

"Expect the worst and you're never disappointed."

"And you also spend your time poised on the edge of life. Hesitation earns you nothing."

"It keeps you safe."

"Safe." She sniffed as if the word were a curse. "That's synonymous with boring in my book."

"But I'm not you."

She was silent for a moment. "I can see I'm getting nowhere."

He studied her calmly, beginning to feel the slightest edge of irritation. "Where was it you wanted to get?"

"It's where *you* need to be that's important. And your place is with Cassandra."

He looked away, shaking his head. How could she be so sure of what he doubted?

Eugenia made a soft sound of disgust. "Well, I'm not going to waste my time when you won't even listen. But remember, when you lose Cassandra this time, it'll be for good." Without giving him a chance to reply, she left, the beads on her navy blue gown flashing as she moved through the crowd.

Daniel took a deep breath and watched her go, wondering how he could lose something he didn't really have. He was brooding on that thought when he glimpsed a familiar face in the crowd of youngsters moving toward the door.

Matt saw him at the same time, and for a moment Daniel thought the boy was going to turn tail and run away. It was to his credit that he didn't. He stopped in front of Daniel. In dress pants, shirt and tie, with his unruly auburn hair neatly combed, he looked very different from the boy Daniel had seen in Cassandra's office over a week ago.

"Hello, Mr. O'Grady," he said.

Daniel nodded. "You did a terrific job in the play, Matt."

"Thanks."

Not wanting to pretend he wasn't still angry with the boy, Daniel continued, "But I was a little surprised to see you. I thought Miss Martin might have thrown you out on your butt."

Not saying a word, Matt hung his head.

Daniel kept his voice stern. "What did you do to worm your way back into her good graces?"

"She's makin' me help her clean up around here every night," Matt muttered. "Some nights we work on my play instead."

"And that's a big struggle, huh?"

"I guess not." Matt looked up and cleared his throat.

"Then why did you tear up her office like you did?"

"I'm sorry for that."

"Being sorry won't always cut it."

"I know."

Remorse was written in every line of Matt's body, and briefly Daniel was the one feeling sorry. This kid was so alone, even more alone than Daniel had once been. Daniel lifted his hand, almost placed it on the boy's shoulder and then remembered how twelve-year-olds hated being treated their age. So he reached into the breast pocket of his jacket instead. "Here, I want you to take my number." He pulled out a business card. "Keep this, so you'll know how to get in touch with me if you need anything."

There was a trace of distrust in Matt's blue eyes as he accepted the card.

Daniel shrugged, deliberately playing it cool. "With you and Miss Martin alone here at night, you might need me sometime."

Matt's shoulders straightened. "I could look after her if there was trouble."

"I know, but keep it just in case. You never know what'll happen."

"Yeah." Very seriously the boy studied the card, then pulled a worn billfold from his pocket and tucked it away.

Daniel decided to push a little more. "You know, Matt, maybe if you and I could go take in a baseball game or something sometime. What do you say?"

The distrust slipped back into his eyes like shades being drawn. Matt backed away. "I don't know about that, Mr. O'Grady, but I'll see you around." He turned and quickly disappeared out the door.

"Nice try."

Daniel recognized the voice as Cassandra's. She stood nearby, her expression soft, full of something like wonder. She said nothing else, and almost immediately someone claimed her attention.

But just that moment was enough to make Daniel suffer more. Eugenia's words began to echo around in his head. *When you lose Cassandra this time, it'll be for good.*

If so, why didn't he just leave and be done with it?

Daniel couldn't have answered that question if his life depended on it. He just stayed. Talking with business associates. Visiting with his sister and Liz and Nathan. Trying, with no success, not to look at Cassandra.

He kept staring.

No matter where Cassandra moved, she could feel Daniel's eyes on her. The sensation soon became annoying. Did he have to glower at her so? He acted as if she had been the one who left here so suddenly over a week ago.

A week. God, it had been horrible. She had jumped every time the phone rang. She had waited for him to show up one night after school. She had even prepared this nice little speech, about how he was right to be so sensible and cautious the other night. She was willing to do almost anything to salvage what they had begun to build. She'd do anything except be the first one to call.

Stupid, damn, foolish pride. How she wished she didn't suffer from it so.

Gradually the crowd began to disperse. Cassandra stood near the door with her staff, shaking hands, speeding people on their way. Finally there were only her friends and Nora and the caterers remaining. And there was Daniel, of course. Most notably, there was Daniel. Wondering why he was sticking around with that disagreeable expression on his face, she sighed.

"You've got to be tired," Nora said. "Why don't you go on home? I'll lock up."

Cassandra shook her head. "You go. I have some things I want to check on."

"I guess that means you won't be leaving with us," Eugenia said, lightly touching the arm of Herbert Black, her escort of this and every recent evening.

"No, I won't."

"Nathan and I will stay with you, Cassandra," Liz said. "He's gone to bring the car round to the front, but we can wait. I don't like you being here at night."

"Absolutely," Eugenia agreed. "Herbert, you and I will stay, too."

Cassandra sighed. "My God, the caterers are still here. What could happen?"

"You never know," Maggie added. "I can stay a half hour or so. I'm picking Don up at the airport, but—"

"Goodness, girls," Mr. Black interrupted in his booming voice. "Can't you just let Daniel stay?"

There was a sudden silence while all eyes swiveled to where Daniel had settled with deceptive calm into a folding chair. Cassandra knew it was deceptive, because she recognized the storm signals in his eyes.

"Yes," he murmured, looking at her. "I'll stay."

Without further ado, Mr. Black began herding Eugenia toward the door. Maggie followed after casting a last, uneasy glance at Cassandra. Only Liz continued to hesitate, and action for which Cassandra was most grateful. She didn't want to be alone with Daniel. She relaxed even more when Liz's husband strolled into the room.

"Somebody waiting for something?" Nathan asked.

"The caterers," Liz explained.

Nathan glanced from Daniel to Cassandra and back to Daniel again. Then he took his wife's hand. "Come on, I think we are what's known as extra baggage."

"But—"

"Come on, we've got better things to do." With a wave of his hand and a flash of his brilliant smile, Nathan started Liz toward the door. And when she tried to protest again, he kissed her.

The gesture wasn't altogether unusual, coming as it did from a man who rarely needed an excuse to kiss his wife. But Cassandra thought there was an unexpected sweetness to the moment. Maybe it was the tender way Liz brushed a tawny lock of hair back from Nathan's forehead. Or maybe it was the way he looked at her, with eyes full of heat and promise. For whatever reason, she felt as if she had opened a door without knocking. And what she saw filled her with envy.

To have what Liz and Nathan had. Would she ever? The question left an ache in her heart.

It didn't help that Daniel's expression held the same wistfulness she felt. Damn him, she thought. It's his choice. Staying in this room with him while in her present mood was more than she could bear. As soon as Liz and Nathan were gone, she murmured an excuse and escaped to her office.

Daniel followed her moments later.

She sensed rather than saw him come into the room. But she kept busy, shuffling through papers, making meaningless notes. She kept pretending not to notice him, until he came around the desk and put his hand on her bare shoulder. Just his touch was scalding. She had to look up at him. And what she saw in his eyes just made her ache some more.

"Please," she murmured. "Just go—"

He shook his head and calmly drew her to her feet. "I'm not going." He brought her hand to his mouth and pressed a kiss in the palm.

Cassandra felt herself swaying toward him. His name was no more than a sigh on her lips.

"I'm not going," he repeated, and there was the beginning of a smile on his lips. "Not tonight. Not without you."

Seven

The lights were low. The gray leather couch was comfortable, and the music on the stereo was a soft, dreamy jazz that matched Cassandra's mood. But what suited her most of all was the company. Daniel sat beside her, and he was in a relaxed, mellow mood. He had shed his jacket and loosened his tie, and he seemed content to sit here forever with his arm around her.

They had said little since that electric moment in her office. The caterers had been dispatched. The school had been locked, and they had driven to Daniel's place without a moment's discussion over the destination. What passed unspoken between them was more important, perhaps easier to understand than words would be. He wanted her with him. She wanted to be there. And now the night stretched in front of them like a long, welcoming road. Cassandra was surprised that she didn't feel more impatient, but like Daniel, she was in no hurry.

"Sure you don't want some wine?" he asked.

She shook her head. "But you should go ahead if you want."

Lazily he trailed a finger from the curve of her shoulder, up her neck to just below her bottom lip. "I don't need anything." The finger brushed across her mouth. "Except what's already here."

Her reaction to his touch was like a shower of rain on a hot summer day. The desire poured through her and then steamed upward, a cycle of want, feeding on itself. Against the finger that still rested on her lips, she lightly touched the tip of her tongue. He drew in his breath sharply and slipped his hand through her hair.

Then he kissed her, cupping the back of her head in his strong steady hands, holding her as if she were a cup of water and he was a man dying of thirst. Just when her pulse had begun to race, he drew away. "You overwhelm me. Did you know that, Cass?"

Though she was trembling with emotion, she managed to smile. "I'm glad."

"That's why I ran out on you last week."

"It was too much?"

"I thought so." He sighed. "The way you make me feel ... well ... I haven't felt that way in a long, long time."

"Maybe it's a habit you could learn to like."

"Maybe."

Belatedly Cassandra remembered the little speech she had prepared and planned to give him if he ever spoke to her again. "You were right to slow it down the other night, though," she began.

He shook his head, giving her a slow smile. "All I did was cause us to waste a whole week, after we've already wasted half of our lives." He kissed her again, hard and direct, momentarily robbing her of coherent thought. "Come on," he whispered, drawing her to her feet. "I don't think I want to waste any more time."

Cassandra placed her hand in his, thinking that she was handing him her heart, as well.

His bedroom was like the rest of Daniel's home, a bold, man's sort of room. Cassandra got the impression of black and gray splashed with red on the bedspread and in the paintings on the wall. The bed was king-size. She had only a moment to study that broad, promising expanse of mattress before Daniel was kissing her, touching her again.

Daniel's patience was gone. Though he willed himself to go slow, to savor every second of what he'd waited so long to know, he couldn't. Not when Cassandra met each of his kisses with an eagerness of her own. Not when her touches betrayed her own impatience.

"Tell me I'm not dreaming," he said as she undid his tie and tossed it aside.

"I don't think so." Her nimble fingers made short work of the buttons on his shirt. Then she pushed the garment off his shoulders and to the floor. Her lips moved from his mouth to his chest as she punctuated her words with kisses. "But Daniel...if this *is* a dream...please don't wake up." In the dim light of the bedside lamp, her grin flashed up at him. "At least not for an hour or so."

"An hour?" he echoed, grinning back. "You're a generous woman, Cassandra Martin."

Her fingers hesitated at the buckle of his belt, then slid downward, cupping him. He grew hard against her hand, and still she smiled her saucy little smile. "I remember you as a generous man, Daniel O'Grady."

His hand closed over hers. "You remember a pig-headed, scared boy."

She shook her head and drew away, suddenly serious. "That's not the way you've been in my memories, Daniel. Not at all."

"Memories either blunt the edges or make them sharper."

"Not always. Some of my memories are crystal clear, and that's why I never stopped wondering what being with you would be like." She stopped and clasped her hands together, as if she were nervous. "Daniel, to clear the air I want to tell you what I did—"

"No." Daniel placed his fingers gently over her lips, silencing her. He didn't want to hear about anyone else. "There's just me and you here tonight, Cass. That's all that matters to me."

"But I was so—"

"Please," he repeated. "I don't want to hear it."

She nodded then, and for a time they stood looking at each other. Then Cassandra stepped back from him again, kicking off her shoes. Her eyes didn't waver from his face as she reached for the zipper at the side of her short black dress. Slowly the zipper went down, inch by slow inch, while Daniel followed its progress with greedy eyes. The dress slid to the floor. Finally. And was kicked aside with Cassandra's usual carelessness. Only then did Daniel allow his gaze to roam up her slender legs.

The sheerest of black stockings were attached to a scrap of red-and-black lace that seemed designed to try a man's patience. Beyond the tempting length of creamy upper leg, a triangle of red lace, unnecessary but delicious nonetheless, shielded the dusk-shadowed delta at the juncture of her thighs. Daniel's gaze slid upward...over her sleek stomach...small waist...full breasts that swelled above a strapless red bra...and finally to her beautifully sweet face.

Her beauty made him catch his breath, although he expelled it just as quickly when her bra joined the dress on the floor.

"Don't," he muttered hoarsely. "Don't take off another thing."

"But Daniel—"

"But nothing." He caught her to him, capturing her lips as his hands swept down to cup her rounded derriere. The lace of her panties was soft to his touch, but softer still was her silky skin. More erotic was the way her breasts flattened against his hair-roughened chest. More hypnotic was the play of her tongue against his own as they kissed. And then there was her scent. Indescribably, completely female. Sexy, with the right mix of mystery. Just that heady fragrance was enough to send him over the edge. But that couldn't happen. Not yet.

Somehow—Cassandra wasn't sure what method of coercion Daniel used—she was eased to the edge of the bed. Then he dropped to the floor and knelt beside her. His hands slipped up her leg...up...up the satiny length of stocking. At the top, his thumb traced over her skin and under the stocking. Over. And under again. And again and again, with spellbinding rhythm.

The simple feather-light touch brought a moan to Cassandra's lips, and she felt herself sinking into the magic of the moment. This was Daniel. This tender, passionate man was the one she had dreamed of, yearned for.

He should have been the first, she thought. She had to swallow the bitter taste of regret that rose to her mouth. Daniel should have been the first to show her how it could be between a man and woman. But wishes wouldn't change the past. What counted was now. And now was simply breathtaking.

With hands braced behind her, she leaned back, closing her eyes as Daniel undid her stocking and rolled it downward with agonizing care. He paused every inch or so to kiss the newly revealed flesh, then repeated the process with the other leg. He didn't stop until the garter belt and panties were gone, as well. And by then, Cassandra was shaking from the force of her desire.

Daniel was trembling, too, and his skin was damp with sweat as they drifted backward on the bed together. But still there was more. More kisses. More moments of mingled sighs and tortured breathing. More time to sate herself in the basic male scent of him, in the feel of his strong, bunching muscles. His mouth, open and wet, drifted to her desire-tightened nipples, and the pleasure built inside her until she had to call out.

He caught the sound with his mouth, and his hands slipped downward, toward the center of her feminine heat. With his first touch, she jerked against his hand.

"No," she murmured, tearing her lips from his. "Please, Daniel, I want you inside me."

Daniel needed little urging. Yet as he stood to strip away his pants and briefs, he hesitated a moment more, stirred by the sight of Cassandra posed so wantonly on his bed.

Cassandra.

In his bed.

Something he could only describe as peace settled alongside the desire that was burning through his gut. This was so very right. The way it should have been long ago.

It was with that thought firmly in mind that he buried himself in the depths Cassandra offered so freely.

One thrust and they went to heaven.

In the time that followed, when sanity gradually returned, Cassandra began to giggle.

"You could do bad things to a man's ego by laughing like that," Daniel protested.

"Well, Mr. O'Grady, it wasn't quite an hour." He groaned, and she laughed harder. "But it was pretty good, considering we waited all these years."

"Pretty good?" Daniel rolled over, carrying her with him so that she was on top. Then he grinned up at her, and golden lights were sparkling in his brown eyes. "If it was only pretty good, I guess we'll have to do it again."

"I guess so," Cassandra echoed, already lowering her mouth to his.

The sound of something—a slamming door, he thought—woke Daniel early the next morning. His eyes flew open, and he panicked for a second, thinking Cassandra was gone. Then he realized she couldn't be gone, because she was lying next to him.

Curled at his side, with one leg thrown over his and one arm draped across his waist, her head was snuggled into his shoulder. That would account for the prickles of pain that were radiating down his arm. Carefully, not wanting to disturb her sleep, he eased away. She stirred but didn't waken, even though she did murmur his name as she settled beneath the covers again. That made Daniel smile. Perhaps she was dreaming of him.

But whatever her dreams were, she looked content, exactly as Daniel felt. They had made love twice—three times? Whatever the number, he shouldn't have such an overwhelming desire for her again. But he did.

Later, he thought, as he turned onto his side to watch her sleep. On the hand resting near her face, she still wore her ruby dinner ring. Even in the weak sunshine that trickled through the blinds, the square-cut stone caught and held the light like trapped fire. Ruby fire.

The ruby earrings she had worn to match the ring were somewhere in the room. She had tossed them away sometime during the night of loving. Her lack of concern about valuable pieces of jewelry was so like Cassandra. Yet he knew she'd never be so careless with this ring.

It had once been Eugenia's ring, and for that reason alone, regardless of its value, Daniel knew how much Cassandra prized it. Eugenia had presented the ring at a high-school graduation party, the same night she had given Liz a pair of diamond earrings and Maggie a single strand of pearls. As one would expect from Eugenia, the gifts were symbolic, representing the difference between her girls. Brilliant Liz. Gentle Maggie. Fiery Cassandra.

Daniel could remember that part clearly. Cassandra had been so excited, ready to start her trek toward stardom, ready to be an adult. Though they were going to separate in the fall—he going back to college, she to New York—on that night, Daniel hadn't believed there was anything that could really come between them. He planned to finish school, move to New York and climb some corporate ladder. Cassandra was going to take Broadway by storm.

But it hadn't worked out the way they planned.

Frowning, Daniel rolled onto his back and lay staring at the ceiling.

It couldn't go wrong again.

They were older. They weren't likely to let a silly argument or disagreement separate them. Remembering the week they had just spent apart, he frowned harder. But he told himself it was different now. Last night had cemented their feelings. And besides, Cassandra wouldn't betray him this time.

Betray. The word twisted through him, scraping against wounds he had never allowed to heal. Perhaps it was time to put away his pain.

Why, he wondered as he'd done a million times before, why did she do it?

He turned toward Cassandra, expecting her to be asleep, and her wide-awake ebony eyes took him by surprise. There was something a little too bright about her smile.

"You're not having regrets already, are you?" she asked as her smile weakened, then disappeared.

He sat up and settled his back against the soft, textured material of the black-and-gray headboard. But he didn't answer her.

Cassandra felt the panic rise inside. "Daniel?" she said, and touched his arm. "There's something wrong. What?"

"I'm just . . ." He paused and thrust a hand impatiently through his sleep-tousled hair. "I guess I'm thinking too much."

Sitting up, Cassandra tucked the sheet under her arms and leaned against the headboard, also. She took a deep breath. "You're thinking about twelve years ago."

He nodded. "Crazy, isn't it? I mean, it doesn't matter in the long run. We were kids—"

"But sex isn't kid stuff."

His smile was wry. "We acted as if it was."

She closed her eyes and leaned her head back. "I used to think you were going to follow me to New York, you know. All that fall, I waited for the telephone to ring, for you to tell me you had forgiven me. When you didn't, I almost called you—a hundred times."

"I probably wouldn't have listened."

"Would you listen now?"

"Maybe it's time to clear the air once and for all."

Cassandra kept her eyes shut. She couldn't look at Daniel and talk about this. "I didn't set out to hurt you," she began. "I just wanted to make you jealous. That's why I went out with—"

"Robby," Daniel supplied with some sarcasm. "Robby Carter."

She shivered. "Please. I've tried to forget his name."

"Forget the name of your first lover? Surely everybody remembers that."

She opened her eyes at his sharp tone.

"I'm sorry," Daniel said, and meant it. "But no matter how old you get or how much you tell yourself it doesn't matter, there are some things that still sting."

Her smile was slight. "Like iodine on a scraped knee."

He touched her cheek. "And losing your girl to someone else, particularly to a low-life scum like Robby Carter."

"You didn't lose me to him."

"I did for a night."

Cassandra closed her eyes again, not wanting to remember. "I don't consider him my first lover," she said softly. "I rarely think of him or of that entire week. It's a black hole in the middle of my life."

Daniel looked away. The week had been dark for him, too. There had been the argument. Their breakup. And Cassandra's date the very next night with a guy he had always despised. Maybe it wouldn't have been so bad if the guy had been anyone other than Robby. But Robby was the kind who couldn't resist boasting of his conquest. So there had been a confrontation and swaggering taunts Daniel couldn't stop, even with his fists. And at last he had seen Cassandra and known the truth just by looking into her eyes.

He had felt like the worst kind of fool, and playing the fool is no small thing to a twenty-year-old who has always been in love with the same girl. A girl who had lost her virginity to someone else.

Beside him, Cassandra shivered and drew the covers up around her shoulders. "It was awful," she murmured, her eyes growing wide and vacant. "The way you looked at me that morning, like I had killed you."

"That's the way I felt."

"I was such a little fool," she murmured. "I just had to prove that I was all grown-up, and if you wouldn't help me prove it, then someone else would do. It was my usual kind of stunt—you know, get my way or be damned." She laughed a little. "The sad part is, it certainly didn't make me a grown-up. I just felt empty."

Daniel brought her close and cradled her against his chest. As he breathed in the sweet scent of her hair, he tried to think of a way to erase all the pain this memory could still bring her. And in wishing that, he realized that for once he was more concerned with what Cassandra felt than with the injustice he thought had been done to him. Even all those years ago when he'd been so sure he loved her, it was himself he had felt sorry for. He had never once considered that she might have regretted what happened.

This was a new experience for Daniel. But maybe, just maybe, it showed he could let go of past disappointments.

"Breaking up with your boyfriend and sleeping with the next available guy is a dumb thing to do," Cassandra murmured.

"I think there were a lot of dumb things done and said that summer. Maybe if I had listened to you—"

"Oh, sure," she said, raising her head to look at him. "Like you were really going to listen to me about my sleeping with another guy. Come on, Daniel. I used to blame it on your not letting me explain, but I don't even know if I understood my reasons back then. All I knew was that you wouldn't do exactly what I wanted."

"And Cassandra always gets what she wants."

"I don't know." She sighed. "I see the same thing every day down at the school. They can't wait to be adults. But they're not so well equipped to take adult consequences." She hesitated and then met his gaze straight on. "Like losing someone you love."

Daniel held her hand against the warmth of his hair-sprinkled chest. "Looks to me as if we've found each other again."

Cassandra wondered for one dizzying moment if he was saying he loved her. Expectantly she held her breath, but he just continued to smile at her. She was unaccountably disappointed, and that was crazy. What an idiot she was to even wonder at his feelings. She was here, wasn't she? Last night had been the most romantic, sensual night of her life. She was nuts to be wishing for more. With that in mind, she pressed a kiss on his mouth and sat back, smiling. "Thanks for coming after me last night. I wasn't going to budge until you did."

"Lucky for me, you looked so damned sexy in your little black dress that I could no longer resist. Of course—" he flashed a wicked grin and tossed the covers back "—you look very nice in nothing at all."

Their laughter lifted and joined in much the same way Daniel brought her body next to his. It was a perfect fit.

Outside, the Sunday morning sun climbed high in the sky and leaked through the open slats in the blinds. It covered the bed in light, warming sheets that needed no more heat than they already contained.

Cassandra called the sunshine an omen. A good one, of course. But then, she had every reason to be hopeful. Little more than a month ago, Daniel had rarely smiled in her direction. Now he was laughing with her in bed.

What else could she want?

The sunshine disappeared that afternoon, and it rained almost every day for the next two weeks. Heavy, ground-drenching thunderstorms. Gentle, sparkling showers. Ditches filled, and gutters worked overtime. And the same people who usually complained about hot dry Augusts moaned about the wet.

In the mornings, Daniel looked out his window at a gray and soggy world. Then he turned around and encountered Cassandra's smile, and everything brightened. Like magic.

He thought he was happy. He told himself he was. He repeated it so often he began to wonder who he was trying to convince. Maybe it was because happiness wasn't something he had wasted too much time worrying about in the past. Despite the problems of his childhood, his adult life hadn't been miserable. Quite the contrary, he had built for himself a pleasant lifestyle. An upscale job. A small circle of friends, who, while not terribly close, could still be relied upon for entertainment and companionship. There had been women in his life, too. Nothing intense, of course, but he hadn't been completely alone all these years without Cassandra. But instead of peaks and valleys, his life had been more like a steady, unwavering line.

The graph had become a little more turbulent with Cassandra around.

She lived life on the edge. Always late. Always with a new idea. Free spirited. Impetuous. Though she had always been this way, she still astounded Daniel with the way she could skip from one activity to the next without missing a beat. Often, of course, the first activity wasn't quite finished when she started the second. That was how she ended up with only chicken in the chicken-and-rice meal she planned. She had plants that were halfway potted and poems that were written except for the last line. And of course, her résumé read like a list of disparate career possibilities instead of well-planned accomplishments. She had tried her hand at many things, but she'd never stayed with any of them long enough to make them work.

And perhaps that was why Daniel couldn't say he was the happiest man on earth. Maybe he was waiting to see if Cassandra would leave him, too. When he was with her, such thoughts were pushed aside by her sunny nature. But when they were apart, when he had time to think, then he wondered and worried.

He was doing just that on a rainy late afternoon as he pulled his car to a halt in front of his sister's house.

His sister's. Daniel smiled at the description. It was his house, too, the house where they had grown up together. Maggie and her husband had been living here when their mother had died. Daniel had expected her to want to sell it after the baby died and her husband departed, but she had stayed on. Perhaps the big old house was her security blanket. Daniel didn't care. He didn't think of this house as home.

As attached as she was to the place, Maggie had seen the wisdom in turning it into apartments. Like most of the older homes on the nice but not quite fashionable street, the house was too much for one person. She and Daniel had pooled their resources to do the remodeling. Now she ran her interior design business and lived on the spacious first floor. The three apartments on the upper two levels brought in a tidy income.

Hurrying through the rain to the front door, Daniel sent an approving glance over the neat look of the house. Maggie's flowers, though soggy, were blooming in the yard, and the white paint and bright blue shutters gave the place a welcoming feel. Certainly it had never looked this nice when their mother had been in charge.

Looking relaxed in jeans and a pink blouse, Maggie met him at the door. "Don't you believe in umbrellas? Or doesn't that fit the macho young executive pose?"

"Cassandra borrowed the umbrella from my car," Daniel explained. "It's the third one she's lost in the past week."

Laughing, Maggie closed the door behind them. "You should know better than to loan her anything. I'm still waiting for a sweater she borrowed in the tenth grade."

Daniel grinned and hung his damp jacket on the foyer's coatrack. "That's just Cassandra for you."

"I wonder what's missing from her gene pool that makes her that way?" Maggie mused as she led the way to the big country kitchen at the rear of the house. This room was her special domain, and as usual it was filled with delicious aromas. Daniel sniffed appreciatively as she lifted the lid on a pot of spaghetti sauce. She had promised him and Cassandra dinner.

He took a seat at the table in the middle of the room, loosened his tie and addressed Maggie's question about Cassandra. "I don't think flightiness is written into her genes. It goes back to the way she was raised. You know as well as I do how her parents were."

Maggie opened the refrigerator and got out a tray of ice. "Oh, Daniel, you blame everything on parents."

"Well, if I'm wrong, then there are millions of psychiatrists out there who have no basis for their entire profession."

Eyebrows raised, Maggie handed him a glass of iced tea.

Holding the cool glass, he leaned back in his chair. "If Cassandra's parents had ever made her finish what she started, she'd be better off today," he insisted. "Most of the time she wasn't punished for doing anything wrong. Then, when they decided to lower the boom, they were too strict."

"You've obviously spent a lot of time dissecting the cause of Cassandra's behavior," Maggie observed in a dry tone.

"It takes some time to understand Cassandra. You have to agree with that."

Maggie again cocked an eyebrow. "Are you saying you understand her now?"

The quiet question took Daniel by surprise. Did he understand Cassandra? "Maybe not," he finally answered and took a sip of tea.

Maggie seated herself across from him and flipped idly through the fabric swatches and notes that littered the table. She was obviously having a hard time coming up with a way to approach him about something. "How is it with you and Cassandra, anyway?" she asked at last.

"It's good. It would be great if..." Daniel caught himself. Putting his doubts into words would make them all the more real.

"If what?" Maggie pressed.

"Nothing."

She touched his hand lightly. "Really, Daniel, tell me."

Why not? he asked himself. Perhaps she could offer some words of reassurance. "It's just what we've been talking about—the way Cassandra never sticks with anything."

"You think the same will apply to you?"

"Maybe. I don't know." He drank some tea, studied the swirling amber liquid in his glass and then looked at his sister. "What do you think?"

Her smile transformed her gentle prettiness into genuine beauty. "You know something? I think this is the first time you've ever asked me for my opinion on anything other than a color scheme."

That made him feel ashamed. This was the one person in the world he should have learned to count on. "I guess I'm mellowing out at last, huh?"

"I like it." Thoughtfully Maggie ran a hand through her short blond curls. "But I wish I could tell you what you want to know, Daniel. Cassandra seems so content right now. I mean she's b—" Maggie stopped herself, biting her lip before she continued, "What I meant is that part of me wants to think she's finally found everything she wants with the school and especially with you. But the other part of me—"

"Just knows Cassandra," he completed for her.

Her brown eyes unhappy, Maggie nodded. "I know that makes her sound so selfish. And she isn't, really. She just doesn't think sometimes. She leaps in. She doesn't consider the consequences. She bites off more than she can chew. Then she bails out. Maybe it does go back to her parents. Perhaps they did make everything too easy for her. She's never had to make hard choices.''

"Not like you and me, huh?" Daniel surprised himself by putting his hand over Maggie's. She threaded her fingers through his and squeezed.

"No," she murmured. "Not like you and me."

They smiled at each other, then Daniel drew away, feeling a bit uncomfortable. Heart-to-heart chats with his sister weren't the norm. Maggie, too, seemed flustered. She got up and made a great show of bustling around the kitchen while he busied himself by glancing through the material on the table. Beneath the fabric swatches were a group of photographs. They were all of the same house, a house he supposed matched the floor plan he found, as well.

"This house is pretty neat," he told Maggie. "New client?"

She wheeled away from the oven where she had just placed a loaf of foil-wrapped bread. "What house?"

Daniel held up the photos. "It's interesting, except that it looks awfully old," he continued, glancing from Maggie's heat-flushed face back to the pictures. "Remodeling it will probably cost a bundle. And the yard looks like it's a wreck." Maggie still said nothing, and Daniel glanced up, puzzled by her silence.

"Maggie, you promised not to tell him."

They both turned to where Cassandra stood dripping in the doorway. "You promised not to," she told Maggie again.

Daniel's glance went from one woman to the other, and he frowned.

Cassandra gulped but then raised her chin. Defiantly. Or so it seemed to Daniel. "Maggie promised not to tell you about my house," she said.

"Your house?" For a moment Daniel didn't understand, but when the realization hit him, his gaze went back to the photographs he held.

Maggie started laughing. "Yes, Daniel," she said, answering his unspoken question. "That house."

Eight

"And through here is the back veranda and the garden," Cassandra said, and prepared to throw the glass-paned door open for Daniel. The drama of the moment was lost, however, when the door wouldn't budge, just as none of the other doors in the house had budged.

Daniel, who had been standing in the middle of the living room gazing at the empty fireplace, laughed humorlessly. "Something wrong with the door, Cassandra?"

"All the doors opened just fine the day I signed the contract. It must be the rain that's making them stick." Jiggling the handle again, she put her weight against the door. It opened then, and she stumbled through to the brick-floored veranda. The step down threw her off balance, and she sat down rather hard on the steps.

Muttering a curse, Daniel came after her. "Cassandra, are you okay?"

"Of course I am," she answered crossly. Then her smile brightened as she looked across the veranda to the wooded lot behind the house, *her* house. She indicated the scene with a sweep of her arm. "See, didn't I tell you this was wonderful?"

Daniel made a sound that could have been agreement as he helped her to her feet. It also could have been disapproval. As she attempted to wipe a smudge of dirt from her red cotton skirt, Cassandra couldn't really tell what he was thinking. "Daniel?" she pressed. "Don't you love it?"

"It looks as if no one has mowed the yard in months."

Cassandra glanced back to the overgrown garden. Maybe it didn't have as much charm as it had on the day two months ago when she had first looked at the house. That day the sun had been shining. That day she had seen all the possibilities. Right now, a foggy twilight was settling over the wet landscape. She had to admit it didn't look as promising as she would have liked. That meant she would have to make Daniel see the magic.

"Imagine it without that pile of leaves and dirt," she told him. "And without half of the bushes and weeds. And without—"

"That's a lot of imagining," he interrupted, and before she could say more he walked back into the house.

"Uh-oh," Cassandra murmured. It wasn't that she had expected Daniel to fall immediately in love with this place, but he wasn't even giving it a chance. All during dinner, when even Maggie had sung the praises of the house, he had grown quieter and quieter. During the tour Cassandra had given him, his comments had been monosyllabic. Now she had the feeling he was going to explode.

Back in the living room, she regarded him warily. "You don't like it, do you?"

He thrust his hands into his trouser pockets, a sure sign he was upset. "I thought the school was going to be your only foray into real estate."

"It was until I saw this house."

"Did you bother to think about it before you signed this contract? I mean, do you even know if you have enough money to pay for it?"

"Of course I know that. And I did think about it."

"For how long? An hour?"

She turned away from his pragmatic questions and back to the view of the garden. But it looked gloomy to her now. Just as the house smelled of mildew and must, something she hadn't noticed until Daniel pointed it out. He was so good at seeing what was wrong with everything. While she was just as good at finding those things that were right. And that applied to more than just a house.

Sighing, she leaned against the doorjamb. Outside, the long summer day was fading fast. The electricity had been turned on in the house, but half of the light fixtures were missing bulbs. That meant the rooms would be pitch-black soon. Cassandra shivered. She'd never been here at night.

Daniel came and stood beside her. "I don't mean to dampen your enthusiasm, Cassandra. Really, I don't. The house has some good points."

"Nice of you to notice," she muttered, feeling spiteful.

He sighed and ran a hand through his hair. "I just hope you've considered what it's going to take to get the place the way you'll want it to be."

"I've considered it."

"It doesn't look as if it's been lived in for a while."

"Three years," she snapped.

"Have any idea why it hadn't sold?"

She pressed her lips together and resolutely stared out the window. "Some people think it's haunted."

"Who told you that?"

"One of the neighbors. She came by one day when Maggie and I were looking things over."

"She say why it's haunted?"

"I don't know if you want to hear that."

Daniel sighed again and let his gaze wander around the big shadowy room. A haunted house. Vacant for three years. Probably the site of a mass murder. He just hoped to God Cassandra had negotiated a terrific price. Because she wasn't going to be able to turn around and sell this sucker any time soon.

"I wish you had talked to me about it," he began.

Cassandra turned on him angrily. "After the way you acted about the school? Good heavens, Daniel, I'm not a glutton for punishment."

"Well, weren't you ever going to tell me you'd bought it?"

She tossed her head. "For your information, I bought it *before* I started consulting you about my every move. Well before we started sleeping together." Even in the fading light, her dark eyes snapped with fury. "As a matter of fact, I don't know that I would have consulted you anyway. Sleeping with me doesn't give you power over all my decisions. I can still do what I want, when I want. And that's exactly what I will do, thank you very much.''

Though controlling Cassandra wasn't really what Daniel wanted, the words struck a little too close to his insecurities, and he reacted with anger. ''What rights does being your lover give me, Miss Martin? Anything other than the obvious?''

She took a step backward. ''Daniel...''

''That's okay,'' he muttered. ''You don't have to strain yourself trying to answer that.'' He turned on his heel. ''Come on, let's get out of here.''

''Daniel, please.'' Cassandra caught his arm. ''I didn't mean to sound as if I don't value your opinion.''

Turning back to her, his expression was still closed and hard. ''Fine. Forget it.''

''No, I'm not going to forget it. Not until you tell me what's really bothering you.''

His angry words rushed out. ''Maybe I'm wondering exactly what's happening between us.''

''What's happening?'' she echoed, puzzled.

''Yeah,'' Daniel murmured. Though he hadn't intended to confront Cassandra with the uncertainty he felt, now he was glad to be getting it out in the open. ''Are we just sleeping together until the newness wears off? Are we working toward something, or is this the culmination? Since you always know what you want to do and when you want to do it, maybe you could give me some direction.''

She regarded him in silence. ''Maybe you could do the same for me.''

Not expecting to have the tables turned on him, Daniel faltered for a moment. ''What do you mean?''

Stepping closer, she raised her chin, as well as her voice. "I mean, do you love me, Daniel O'Grady?" The words rang through the empty house, echoing in an eerie hollow fashion.

He did love her, of course. He had never really stopped. But he hadn't planned on saying the words like this, with both of them angry.

"What's wrong?" she said, her voice just a nuance away from taunting. "Are you waiting for me to say it first? Is it safer that way?"

How does she know that? he wondered. *How has she always been able to read every emotion I try to hide?* "No matter who admits it first, there isn't anything safe about being in love," he said finally, after the silence between them had stretched to its breaking point.

"And how do you know that?"

He stepped forward, taking her hands in his. "Because I've been in danger since a summer day when you were thirteen."

"Oh, Daniel." His name was a sigh that she smothered against the summer tweed of his jacket. Her arms stole around his neck as she lifted her face upward. His love found affirmation in the lips she pressed to his. "Say it," she murmured against his mouth. "Say you love me again."

"I love you again."

He could feel the laughter that went through her, but when her eyes met his, they were very serious. "I love you, too." She kissed him. "Again. Always. You didn't really doubt that, did you?"

Daniel could have told her about a multitude of doubts, ones that couldn't be assuaged by the exchange of a few, however meaningful, words. For like the streetwise prince in Matt's morbid play, he had always lost those he loved, even those who said they loved him. He needed more than words before he would believe Cassandra was really and truly his. But exactly what that proof would be, he couldn't say. And maybe all the proof he needed was having her in his arms. Though doubts still nibbled at him, he went for the obvious.

"I want to make love to you," he said, framing her face in his hands.

"Let's go home."

"No, here."

Cassandra looked around the darkened room, her eyes widening. "You're kidding?"

"It's your house. Don't you want to christen it?"

"Don't you think some champagne cracked over the mantel would be more appropriate?"

He kissed her nose. "Afraid of ghosts, Cassandra?"

That brought her chin up. "I'm not afraid of anything."

She lied, of course. Cassandra admitted that but only to herself. It wasn't ghosts that frightened her. It was the strength of what she felt for Daniel. She had never allowed herself to become so entangled with any other man. And there had been other men in the past twelve years. Not many. After what had happened the summer she and Daniel parted, she had become very selective. The men she had known had been special. But not one of them could touch her soul the way Daniel did.

It wasn't just the sex. She told herself that even as Daniel's mouth and hands slid over her body, seeking a reply to his sensual requests. Yes, the sex with Daniel was fabulous, all-consuming, relentlessly passionate. But she knew it wouldn't be that way if they weren't soul mates. Though she had never completely subscribed to the notions of predestination and fate that had captured so many of her friends' imaginations, Cassandra knew in her heart that she and Daniel had been matched, one to the other, long before either of them had realized it on their own.

Outside, a new shower of rain swept across the veranda and tapped against the door with watery fingers. Perhaps ghouls danced in the shadows in the corners of the room. Cassandra heard whispers in the wind that chased down the chimney, and briefly, she shivered in the draft. But for the most part she saw nothing, heard nothing, felt nothing but what built between them.

They undressed quickly, with fingers fumbling in the dark, hands reaching to help, eager to know the feel of skin against skin. On Daniel's lips, Cassandra tasted love, tender yet mixed with desperation. She wondered why he would be desperate when to have all she had to offer required just a touch, just a word. She sought to turn that desperation into satisfaction, to anticipate his needs.

Her hands traveled the solid planes and angles of his body, skimming through the crisp furring of hair on his chest, lingering where his arousal grew harder. As they sank to the cushion made by their discarded clothes, she became bolder. And her mouth retraced the journey of her fingers. Skimming. Lingering. In all the same places.

The intimacy of that action made Daniel catch his breath and turned his voice into a hoarse rasp. "I could die this very minute."

"Not yet," Cassandra murmured as she slid once more up his body. "If you have to go, take me with you."

He smelled like rain, she decided, burying her face in his chest. Like rain and soap and some unnameable scent that was merely male. She drew in the smell while her tongue encircled a flat male nipple. It pebbled against her wet caress, and Daniel jerked beneath her.

He dragged her lips up to meet his. Wild, hot and frenzied, the kiss set off rockets inside her. His hands were in her hair, against her breasts, across her belly, in the dewy softness between her legs. It seemed to Cassandra that he stroked every inch of her flesh, sparking fire with each touch. She was burning up, soaked with sweat and more than ready.

So gently, firmly, she slipped astride his lean hips and guided him deep inside her.

He came off the floor to meet her.

Heart to heart. Face-to-face. They rocked together.

"My God," Daniel whispered, burying his face in the hollow between her breasts. He thrust upward. Deeper. "Cassandra. God, how I love you, Cass."

Muscles stretching like a bow, he arched ever higher. Again and again he reached his target. Until the climax broke through her with shattering force. He joined her then, saying her name over and over, so that finally the word curled through her with the same force as the last urgent threads of excitement.

They fell back on the hard wooden floor as if it were the softest of feather beds. Then they lay together, bodies close, minds closer still. In the silence and darkness there was only the sound of their gradually calming breaths and the tap-tap-tap of the rain against the porch.

"I guess the ghosts got a show," Cassandra finally murmured, giggling softly.

"I doubt that they minded."

"Maybe we chased them away."

She heard Daniel draw in a deep breath. The sound was full of contentment. "I sort of like this house," he said after a pause. "Even if it is haunted."

Snuggling close to his side, she combed her hand through the perspiration-dampened hair of his chest. "I like it, too. I liked it the minute I came up the driveway. Something inside me just said this is home."

Daniel settled her head beneath his chin. "Why did you come home, Cass? Why come back to Nashville? You never had plans to be a teacher."

"Now, how do you know that? Maybe it's been a secret yen of mine all these years."

"Really, tell me what brought you back. I thought you loved New York."

"I did. I do."

His hand brushed over her back, back and forth with a steady, calming rhythm. "Then why'd you leave?"

"I got a stale bagel."

The rhythm of his hand stopped.

"I know it sounds silly, but every morning that I was in New York, I stopped at the same deli for a fresh hot bagel with cream cheese. It was always perfect. The coffee was always hot. I could sit by the window, usually with a friend or two, and read the paper and watch that big city come to life. I loved it."

"So maybe the cook had a bad morning?"

"I don't know." She sighed. "All I know for sure is that on a morning last November I went to that deli and ordered my usual breakfast. The bagel was stale. The coffee was too strong. None of my friends were there. And I felt so homesick. That's when I got the idea for the school."

Realizing she was dead serious, Daniel shook his head. "You didn't have the idea before that?"

She kissed his chin. "Nope. It came to me right then and there, on a cold, yucky New York morning. Just think what might have happened if that bagel had been fresh."

Just think, Daniel repeated to himself. If Cassandra hadn't had a whim over breakfast, this summer wouldn't have happened. *They* wouldn't have happened.

He wondered what would happen the next time someone tampered with her favorite foods. And he wondered if it would be him, and not a city or delicatessen, who was left behind.

Daniel was grateful for the cover of darkness in the room. Otherwise, Cassandra might have seen how it bothered him that she could make bold decisions on the strength of a notion. He didn't want her to see that it upset him. She would just make more promises, and he would have more to lose the next time she changed her mind.

As if his heart weren't already on the line. If she broke that heart again, what would he have left?

"I'm glad you like my house," she drawled. "I was sort of planning on spending some time with you here. This fall maybe we could heat up the fireplace. How does that sound? Maybe pretty good, huh?"

He didn't want to answer, but he seemed to have little choice in the matter. So he muttered a noncommittal, "Maybe so."

"Well, don't act so excited about it," Cassandra teased. "Repairs are starting Monday. I'm supposed to move in in a month."

"Terrific."

She was quiet for a moment. "Daniel?"

"Yeah."

"Are you okay?"

Don't mind me, he wanted to say. *I'm just putting some fences around my heart. They won't help, but they sure won't hurt, either.* But, instead, he muttered a terse, "We need to go."

He was silent on the drive back to Maggie's to pick up Cassandra's car, and once there he made up an excuse about going back to the office. Cassandra headed to his place, as usual. He wanted to ask her not to, but he could think of no reason to give her.

So he went to his office and sat brooding over the financial reports of a company Mr. Black was thinking of buying. The reports could have waited, which was just as well since Daniel made no headway on them. All he could see was Cassandra.

"Goddamn silly woman," he muttered, ripping a page from the legal pad he was using. He crushed the paper in his fist.

"Stupid, stale bagels." With that the paper went flying across the room, landing at the feet of Wally, the night security guard.

"You look to be working hard, Mr. O'Grady," the man said, bending down to retrieve the paper.

Daniel's laugh was short. "Not working at all is more like it."

The man shook his graying head as he leaned against the doorjamb. "Haven't seen you much lately. You must have worked out that problem you had."

Daniel frowned, not understanding.

"You know, that woman problem you were having back a month or so ago."

Then Daniel remembered talking with Wally on the first night Cassandra had waltzed into his life again. He leaned back in his chair. "I don't know that my problems with this particular woman are ever going to end."

Wally chuckled. "A feisty one, eh?"

"Tell me something. How are you ever really sure of them?"

"Ask me an easy one—like how we erase the national debt. That would be an easier, shorter answer, even though hundreds of elected officials can't figure it out."

"So what you're saying is you're never sure."

"I didn't say that," Wally returned. "I'm sure of my Margaret. Been sure of her for forty years. But don't ask me exactly how it came to be. Or why. Or exactly when it happened."

"That's not very reassuring."

The older man drew away from the door and hitched his trousers up, all the while shaking his head. "If you were to ask me what I think, Mr. O'Grady, I'd say you'd come closer to finding your answers if you were with the lady in question instead of here at the office."

Daniel grinned wryly. "Maybe you're right."

"Once you see her, you might not have a problem at all."

Daniel repeated that all the way home. He kept it in mind when he found Cassandra waiting on the couch, wearing lace and silk and a sleepy, sexy smile. He almost believed it when for the second time that night they found each other in the darkness.

With her silk nightgown pushed to her waist and her body warm and pliant beneath his own, Cassandra was enough to convince him of most anything. At least for the night.

Unfortunately, the morning came. And with it came all his doubts.

How could it last? he wondered. Cassandra had never stuck with anything in her life. He wasn't fool enough to think he'd be the exception.

"You want these in here, Miss Martin?"

Distractedly Cassandra glanced up from her desk. Matt stood in the doorway, and he held a box of what looked to be paper for the copier machine.

"A man delivered it downstairs," he explained.

"He should have brought it up here."

"That's okay." The boy's face was red, and he was puffing a bit from the exertion of carrying the box upstairs. "It's not heavy. I can handle it."

Cassandra hid her smile. Matt was always trying to impress her. "Well, you can put it over here in the storage closet," she said as she got up to open the door for him. With great restraint, she managed not to ask him if he needed her help. She knew he would refuse it.

"Thanks," she said. She returned to her desk, but still he lingered near the doorway. "Got something on your mind, Matt?"

"No." He shoved his hands into his pockets. "I mean, yes . . . I guess."

Cassandra sat back in her chair and smiled at him patiently. He always had such a hard time asking questions. It was as if he expected no one to pay any attention to what he said. She nodded to the chair in front of her desk. "Take a seat, and tell me what you need."

He chose to stay by the door, where he shifted nervously from one sneakered foot to the other. "I was wondering if I had to stop helping you around here once school starts."

"Oh, so you like doing the dirty work, do you?"

He grinned at her. "Not really. But I figure I still owe you for . . ." His gaze went to the shelf of plants in front of the window, and the smile disappeared.

Cassandra shook her head. "I think you've repaid me, Matt. The cleaning crew has only come in once a week since you started helping out. That saved the school a bundle of money."

"So don't you still need me? I could just stick around, you know. Mr. O'Grady doesn't like it when you're here alone at night."

"Is that what Mr. O'Grady told you?"

"Yes, ma'am."

When was this? Cassandra wondered. Daniel hadn't been by the school in nearly two weeks. Deliberately she forced that annoying thought to the back of her mind, just as she'd been doing for days.

"Miss Martin?"

She looked into Matt's serious blue eyes and realized she had been drumming her fingers impatiently on the desk. "I'm sorry, Matt. I guess I'm kind of distracted today."

He began to edge out the door. "That's okay. I can come back some other time."

"No, you don't have to do that," she said. "But about this helping out around here—won't it get in the way of your homework?"

"No, ma'am."

"What does your mother think?"

His eager face darkened and fell. "She doesn't care," he mumbled.

Cassandra gazed at his bowed head in concern. There had been a lot of improvement in Matt's attitude in recent weeks, and there had been no further violent outbursts. He was getting along with the other students, and he had even started to work on revising his play. Nora gave the credit for his change solely to Cassandra, saying it was amazing what a schoolboy crush could do for a problem kid. Whatever the reasons, Cassandra was glad he had learned to control his runaway emotions. But he was still a troubled boy, and she was sure the trouble came from home. In the long run it would probably be better for Matt if he continued to spend more time here.

"Have your mother write me a note," she said after some consideration. "If she says it's okay, you can stay late on the two nights when I have classes with the older kids. And of course, you'll still be coming for your own classes."

The boy bit his lip and hesitated before asking, "Can I tell my mother I'm still being punished?"

She stared at him in surprise. "Whatever for?"

"That way I know she'll write the note."

What telling logic, Cassandra thought as she started to say no. But she couldn't find it in her heart to disappoint him. "You just bring me a note, Matt. I won't worry too much about why your mother thinks you're here."

"Gee, thanks." Eyes sparkling, he left.

Wondering if she had done the right thing, Cassandra turned back to the schedule she had been double-checking. Hard as it was to believe, school really would be starting next week. That meant more night work. And less time with Daniel.

"Just when I need to spend more time with him," she muttered.

She wished she knew what was bothering him. Ever since that evening at her house, he had been acting differently. She couldn't understand it, either. They were in love, weren't they? So why was he so remote all of a sudden? It felt as if the only time they really connected was in bed. And as much as she enjoyed that connection, she wanted more than that with Daniel. Dammit, they'd *had* more than that. So what was bugging him?

The questions made her head ache. As did the paperwork on her desk. How did it pile up this way? Maybe it was because she hated it so much. Working with the kids brought her immense satisfaction, but the details that went along with the school's operation...God, they drove her crazy.

She covered her face with her hands, hoping the mess on her desk would magically disappear. But when she looked again, her eyes were drawn straight to the calendar. It had been exactly six months since she had opened the school.

It seemed more like yesterday.

And at the same time, an eternity ago.

Groaning, she put her head all the way down on the desk. Problems, problems, problems. That's all she had.

What was wrong with Daniel?

And with her?

The sound of the telephone ringing was like a lifeline. She grabbed the receiver.

"Goodness," Eugenia said. "You must be waiting for a call."

Thinking back to the days when every call could be from a casting director or a modeling agency or a recording studio, Cassandra sighed. "I wish."

"My, but we're down in the dumps today, aren't we?"

"And I need to be cheered up." Deliberately Cassandra swiveled her chair away from her paperwork. Perhaps that way she wouldn't feel so guilty. "How about lunch?"

"Exactly the reason I was calling. Liz and Maggie have already said yes. How about in a half hour?"

Feeling instantly better, Cassandra agreed and hung up. As she grabbed her purse from a desk drawer, she felt a pang of remorse. Or maybe it was just a twinge. Whatever the case, she didn't dwell on it for long.

She needed to accentuate the positive. That shouldn't be too tough since that was what she excelled at. She would think about all the good things that had happened between her and Daniel. She would have a long lunch and order a luscious dessert, and afterward she would go for a drive around the city. That would blow the cobwebs from her brain.

Some good, bracing wind in her face always helped. She could remember the time in London when the producer who had promised her a recording contract had assembled a group of songs she couldn't stand. She had felt immensely better after going for a stroll along the Thames.

Afterward, she had strolled right over to the airport and caught a plane to New York.

But she wouldn't think about that now. She would concentrate on forgetting her cares.

And maybe while she was gone, some little elves would clear her desk.

And suggest to Daniel that he marry her.

On that happy note, Cassandra closed her office door.

Nine

———

I don't think I like being a grown-up," Cassandra announced.

Two of the three women at her table stopped their conversation to stare at her. But Liz didn't even look up from the dressing she was adding to her salad. "Who says you're a grown-up?"

"My desk does." Disgusted, Cassandra cupped her chin in the palm of her hand.

"Talking desks," Eugenia observed. "That doesn't sound very grown-up to me."

"It's not really the desk, but more what's on it."

"Bills?" Maggie asked.

Cassandra nodded. "And insurance forms and schedules and God-knows-what else."

"Well, it does sound like a grown-up's desk," Liz said.

"Maybe I'll hire an assistant," Cassandra mused.

Maggie tsk-tsked. "You could just buckle down and get it done, you know."

Cassandra made a face, and a chuckle made its way around the table.

Then Eugenia's eyebrows drew together in a frown. "I certainly hope you're not wasting the money Herbert invested in your school, Cassandra."

"Of course not. Daniel rides herd on that."

"Sounds as if Daniel should be riding herd on the whole operation," Liz commented. "Why don't you ask him for some help?"

"And have him say I told you so?" Shaking her head, Cassandra morosely prodded the spinach leaves on her plate. What she didn't say was that Daniel was mad at her about something. They probably wouldn't think that was anything out of the ordinary, either.

Thoughtfully Maggie stirred sweetener into her cup of coffee. "Cassandra, what I'd advise you to do is get busy and get the work out of the way. That's how I take care of things I don't enjoy doing. You'll feel much better afterward."

Cassandra couldn't imagine how such a task could make her feel anything but bored. She was beginning to wish she had never brought up the subject of her work, for she was getting no sympathy from her friends. Instead of helping, lunch was making her feel more restless than she had before.

A touch on her arm made her look up at Liz. "Welcome to the real world," her friend murmured. "The grown-up world."

Is this all there is? Cassandra asked herself, paraphrasing an old song. If so, she . . . what? What in the world did she want, anyway?

Her planned drive helped a little. It was refreshing to feel the August sun on her face. She rolled down the window and turned up the radio. The crashing guitars and driving drums of a rock and roll hit matched her mood. So did the smell of automobile exhaust and the blast of impatient horns. They reminded her of New York. If there had been a hot dog stand at the corner near the school, the image would have been complete.

At least there were the kids. She lost herself in her afternoon class and could have called the afternoon a complete success if it wasn't for the desk full of work that was still waiting in her office. Refusing to consider it, she stayed down in the theater, seated on the edge of the stage. She studied the scenery the stage crew was assembling for the fall production of *Romeo and Juliet*. Once upon a time, she had played Juliet. And earned six curtain calls.

Daniel found her sitting like that, her eyes wide and dark, her lips set in a discontented line. He couldn't help wondering what she was regretting.

"Are you trying to decide if the balcony scene will work?" he asked quietly. "Or just pondering the state of the world?"

She looked up at him and blinked, as if she had to come from a distant corner of her mind to greet him. But her warm, sweet smile was gratifying.

"Hello, stranger," she drawled. "It's been a while since you moseyed into these parts."

He had been staying away from the school. He had no good reason, really, except that every moment he spent with Cassandra bound him harder to her. "I've been busy, working on Mr. Black's latest acquisition," he lied.

"I know." She sighed and looked down while her fingers nervously pleated the material of her saucy red skirt. "Working late nights, not waking me up when you come in."

The dissatisfied note in her voice touched his heart. He stepped toward her. "You miss me?" he whispered.

Her eyes held a promise. "You know I do."

"Good."

She held out her hands to him. "Got some special reason for coming round here?"

"Yeah. This." Ignoring her outstretched hands, he caught her in his arms instead, and as he lifted her from the stage, he lowered his mouth to hers.

"That's much better," she murmured when her feet finally touched the floor. "Much, much better."

His fingers tangled in the black glory of her hair, and he saw that despite his kisses, she still wore an air of discontent. "Something wrong?"

She shook her head, lying, he was sure. All she would say was, "Take me dancing."

"Now?"

"If not sooner. I've got all kinds of work to do, and I don't want to do it. I just want to go dancing with you."

Daniel had been up to her office and seen her desk before Matt had told him she was in the theater. So he knew she wasn't lying about her work. And he knew the sensible thing might have been to go upstairs and help her wade through the mess. But that wasn't what she wanted. That wouldn't clear the unhappiness from her eyes.

So he took her dining and dancing. He had never pretended to be a dancer, but he felt pretty damn good with Cassandra in his arms. They gazed into each other's eyes like two romantic fools. Swaying together. Even when breaking apart would have better suited the music, Daniel held on to her. Tight. And when they were home, he made love to her as if it were the first time—or the last. He wasn't sure which description better suited his mood.

Yet the next day, her restlessness was back.

And the day after that, too.

Daniel wondered then if this was how the end began—with him trying to satisfy some need she wouldn't or couldn't even tell him about.

He hoped not. God, how he hoped not.

On Thursday afternoon Cassandra sat in her office, remembering how it felt to dance with Daniel. The memory actually made her smile, even as she filled out some long-neglected insurance forms. Maybe they should go dancing every night. Maybe then she could ignore the way he watched her all the time. As if he were expecting bad news, or something.

Even as the thought occurred to her, she told herself not to be silly. She was imagining things, making trouble where there was none. Daniel was coming by after her late class to take her to dinner. There was no need to worry about him. Just because it hadn't worked out before. Just because nothing she ever did lasted . . .

"No." She halted the treacherous flow of her thoughts with that one word. Then, thankfully, the ringing telephone demanded her attention.

Almost an hour later, when she finally hung up the phone, the entire world had changed. And she was dancing around her office.

A part. An honest-to-God wonderful part in a wonderful play. And they wanted her. *Her.* Wait till she told Eugenia, and Liz and Maggie. And Daniel. Of course she had to call him right now.

Daniel.

Thinking of him, Cassandra's hand faltered on the telephone. She sank down into her desk chair. He might not be too keen on her leaving for New York. But it wasn't for forever. And the school...

The school.

God, for one wild and crazy minute she had completely forgotten the school and her classes and the kids and the staff. She couldn't abandon them. She didn't want to abandon them.

But this part. This wonderful, wonderful part.

"There has to be a way," she muttered. "There has to be a way for me to do everything."

Figuring out a way to have everything and do everything she wanted was what Cassandra did best. It didn't matter that she had never been really successful in executing her ideas. It was the planning that was her strong suit.

Accordingly she had it all figured out by the time Daniel came to the school that night.

He was early. He slipped into his usual place in the darkened back row of the theater, and as always, she instantly knew he was there. Her nerves, already stretched to the outer limits, felt as if they would snap in two.

Daniel was going to be happy for her, she told herself. He would agree to her plan. He would kiss her and put her on the plane himself.

That image had seemed sane and reasonable when she had been sitting alone in her office. It didn't feel that way when she faced him in the empty theater after the class.

But, taking a deep breath, she plunged ahead, anyway.

And Daniel's first reaction was too sane, too unshakably frozen.

A mask settled over his face. An unreadable, uncrackable mask. The same mask he had worn all these terrible years when he had been hating her. "You're leaving?" was all he could say.

"No, that's not what I said," she returned, growing more nervous by the minute. "I said I was going to New York to do a play."

"And that's not leaving?"

"Not for good. Like I just told you, I'm going to hire someone to take over the school. I'll fly in at least every two weeks to check on things and to see you. And you can come up on the other weeks. We'll see each other all the time."

"No, we won't."

Ignoring his tight, clipped words, she rushed ahead. "It's just too good a part to turn down, Daniel. One of my friends—I told you about him—we used to have breakfast together—"

"Stale bagels," Daniel muttered and, if possible, his eyes became colder, the lines beside his mouth more distinct.

"That's right," Cassandra said, faltering. "And I know how wonderful his play is. It's like a dream come true that it's finally going to be staged. Off-Broadway. But with good backing. The director is someone I've worked with, too. And he wants me. *Me*, Daniel. Isn't that terrific? Isn't that—"

"It's damn wonderful." He spat the words at her, and Cassandra took a step backward.

"I thought you'd be happy for me—"

"Happy?" Daniel wondered that even Cassandra could be so dense. *Happy?* Oh, sure. That was why he wanted to kick a hole through the wall and run till he dropped in his tracks. Yeah, it was happiness that was burning right through the bottom of his gut. *Happy?*

"Daniel—"

He waved her concern aside, and then because he was tempted to shake her until her teeth rattled, he thrust his hands hard into his pockets. Some primal urge deep inside him had wanted to shake her before. But not like now. For the first time in his life, he really understood why one person might physically harm another. When all you could see was bright red fury, you were capable of sudden violence.

She was leaving. Leaving. How could she do it?

Cassandra couldn't know the depths of his anger. If she had, she wouldn't have put her hand on his arm. With a savage oath—words he had never used with Cassandra—Daniel jerked away. "Don't," he growled from between clenched teeth. "Don't touch me, Cassandra."

Her expression changed then, from beseeching to wary. "Daniel, I don't know why you're so upset. We can work things out."

"Oh, yeah, your twisted little mind has worked this all around, hasn't it?"

"Twisted?"

"Yes. Twisted and selfish."

Now anger edged into her voice. "I should have known you wouldn't listen to me. I thought you were different, changed, that you could see things from another person's point of view—''

"You mean go along with whatever scheme you dream up?''

"Stop putting words into my mouth," she said, and turned away. "I'm not going to discuss this with you until you're ready to listen to reason.''

Before he realized his own intent, he caught her arm and spun her back to face him.

"Daniel," she protested, pulling away.

"What's wrong?" he challenged. "Can't stand to face how I really feel? Is my reaction different than the way you fantasized it would be? Oh, my, how terrible, the whole world's not jumping when Cassandra snaps her fingers.''

His sharp, cruel words were cutting close to the truth, and Cassandra couldn't stand to listen to them. Again she tried to walk away. Again he hauled her back to him. And this time he held her tight to his chest. So close she could feel the rapid pounding of his heart. So close she couldn't miss the anger and hurt that warred in his eyes.

"No," he muttered. "You're not going to do this to us." He kissed her then, a punishing kiss. With nothing of love or gentleness about it. His lips merely branded hers. The hands he passed over her body did much the same thing.

"What was I?" he muttered against her mouth. "Just someone to warm your bed during your little sojourn here?''

She twisted her face away from his. "Daniel, don't—''

"Don't what? Don't worry about who'll keep you warm in New York?''

"That's not fair."

"There was nothing fair about the last time you left me and crawled into someone else's bed."

And so the past reaches out and slaps me again, Cassandra thought, as he forced another brutal kiss on her mouth. It wouldn't do any good to try to correct his assumptions. Hurt beyond measure, she endured his loveless caress until he finally set her free.

She backed toward the door while Daniel stared at her with eyes that pierced straight to her soul.

"I knew you'd do this," he whispered. "I knew you couldn't last. Not for me. Not for this school. Damnation, Cassandra, how does it feel to be running out on everyone who needs you?"

"I'm not running out," she protested again. "Daniel, please. I have to go do this. I have to go prove something to myself."

He came toward her again, and she could see that the hurt had won over the anger in his gaze. "I thought you were proving something with me." The muscles in his jaw worked hard. "Cass, I thought you had come home."

Uneasily Cassandra thought of her house, of the excitement that had fired the start-up of the school. She *had* thought she was home. No, she *was* home. But she had to go do this. She had to. She repeated the words to herself like a naughty child writing the same phrase over and over again on a blackboard. And yes, she thought, with desperation, she did believe the words. Yes, she had to go.

"Daniel, performing is my love."

"I thought I was."

The breathless note in his voice brought her back toward him. "You are—"

"I thought this school was, too. What about that dream, Cassandra?"

"I won't lose it."

He shook his head. "I don't buy that. The school won't last without you here. It's *your* school, remember? Your vision. The one you told me was making a difference—"

"But I have to go, Daniel. I have to." Cassandra didn't realize how loud her voice had become until she heard the echo that chased around the theater. She started to run from the wild, desperate sound.

And that was when she saw Matt.

She had forgotten that he was still in the building, but it was his night to do the cleanup. He stood just inside the theater, holding one of the swinging doors open. He stared at her, eyes round and blue and as wounded as Daniel's. There was no telling how much of the argument he had heard. "Matt—"

"You're going away, aren't you?" The words were more accusation than question.

Cassandra nodded, going toward him slowly. Like Daniel, he had to understand that she was coming back. "I'm going to do a play—"

"But you're leaving."

"Not for good—"

"And Mr. O'Grady said the school would close."

"That's not true."

"What did I do?" the boy demanded.

"You didn't do anything, Matt."

"But you're leaving." His adolescent voice rose and cracked on the last word. "What did I do to make you go?"

The prince in his play, Cassandra thought bleakly, the one who lost everything and everyone. To Matt, her leaving was simply another scene. She felt, rather than saw, Daniel come up behind her.

"Matt," he said calmly. "This has nothing to do with you."

"But everyone goes when I'm bad."

Cassandra thought she knew what had him confused. "Matt, your father didn't die because of you."

"That's not what she said."

"She?" Daniel pressed.

Tears streamed down the freckled face. "Mother told me to be quiet so Dad could rest. But I wasn't quiet. And he died."

"It wasn't your fault," Cassandra insisted. "He had a heart attack."

"No, I was bad!" the boy screamed. "And when you're bad, she takes things away. That's why he died. Because of me! Why are you going, too?"

"Matt, please...Matt!" Cassandra's explanation was lost in the swinging of the doors. Clearly Matt didn't want to hear her reasons for leaving, and though they followed him, he was already gone, just like the last time.

In the humid early September night, outside the school's front doors, Daniel faced her. "Well," he said. "I guess this will give you something to think about on the plane to New York."

And then he was gone, too.

It was a long time before Cassandra turned out the lights on the first floor of the school. A long time before she went up to her office. She turned the window air conditioner up until it roared in defense against the night's sticky heat. Then she switched off the lights

here, too. Somehow the darkness was more suitable
for the thinking she had to do.

She avoided those thoughts as long as she could. She
almost called Matt's mother to see if the boy had gotten home all right. Then she reconsidered. She didn't
want to get him in trouble with the ''she'' he had spoken of with such fear. My God, what had his mother
done to him? Tomorrow Cassandra had to do something about his situation. She had to do that much
before she left for New York.

If she left.

The *if* nibbled at the back of her mind like a pesty
fly. She kept swatting it away.

She'd give anything if Matt hadn't heard the argument between her and Daniel. She was sure if she
could have told him she was leaving in her own time
and in her own way, he wouldn't have taken it so hard.

Perhaps she was just fooling herself.

She had made herself a part of that boy's life. It was
a responsibility she had taken on willingly, despite the
counselor's worries that Matt was growing too de-
pendent on her, despite Daniel's admonishments that
she was getting in too deep. Matt needed her, and she
had let him down.

Just as she had let Daniel down.

Again.

Why hadn't she realized he would take her going to
New York as another betrayal? Now, with a cool head,
she could see the folly in the plan she had devised.
Long-distance relationships were okay for some people. But not for Daniel. He needed the day-to-day
commitment. A solid base. Maybe it was because he
had never had that as a child. But whatever the reason, a commuting romance wasn't his style.

To him, she had been leaving him for good.

Just as his father had eventually left his family.

Just as Cassandra had left him once before.

No wonder he had reacted with rage. She could forgive him that brutal kiss and his hurtful words now. It made sense that he would strike at her.

But understanding how he felt didn't tell her what she should do.

What did she want?

She tried concentrating on the part she had been offered. She knew the character so well, having read it in each stage of the writer's development. She knew it was a part that was made for her. A new play. It would be thrilling.

She could close her eyes and taste the excitement there would be on opening night. She could feel the makeup on her face, see the bright rows of footlights. For a couple of months, she'd be in heaven on earth. The feeling might go on forever if the play moved to Broadway. If she got great reviews. If some other director saw her and cast her in some other play. Or a movie.

Broadway. Hollywood. Success. Cassandra had made that imaginary trip a million times. The reality turned on something as intangible as one critic's reaction to one night at the theater. It was a flimsy basis on which to place one's hopes.

For it was just as likely the play would fold within weeks. And soon she could be sitting in a delicatessen, eating a stale bagel and wishing she was having tea with Eugenia.

Or making love with Daniel.

When she had come home last year, Daniel hadn't been part of the picture. Perhaps there was a vague

hope that he would stop hating her. Maybe somewhere in her secret heart she had wanted to explore
what they had left unfinished years ago. But she
hadn't staked her future on it. She had invested her
dreams in this school.

Daniel had been an unexpected bonus. But now it
seemed her very life depended on him. His smile was
what got her started in the mornings. His arms around
her could make even the most boring day special.
Daniel was solid, someone to hold on to when nothing was going her way. He was the base on which she
could build everything else in her life.

For the first time in Cassandra Diane Martin's
roller-coaster-ride life, she had been doing something
right. So what if she hated the school's paperwork? So
what if there were days when she wanted to scream at
the routine? Those were the days when Daniel could
take her dancing. There were just as many other days
when she was astounded by some teenager's raw, un-
polished talent. Days when she read a play such as the
one Matt had written and saw the promise that was
waiting to bud. Ups and downs. Ordinary days. Ex-
traordinary ones.

"The real world," she whispered, thinking of what
Liz had said to her. For a while there, it had looked as
if Claire and William Martin's spoiled little brat had
finally grown up.

Why would she want to trade that for a nebulous
Broadway-bound dream?

She made her choice.

Why? she wondered. Why did it suddenly seem like
such a simple decision?

She had to get to Daniel. She had to tell him, convince him that he could count on her.

It was when Cassandra started to get up that she smelled the smoke.

It was when she switched on her desk lamp that she saw the thin gray stream rising through the gap beneath her door.

But even then, as fear clamped over her like some monstrous set of jaws, all she could think of was Daniel.

Ten

From Daniel's patio he had a beautiful, unobstructed view of a row of condominiums just like his own. Until tonight that view had never bothered him. Tonight he wished for mountains or a lake or even a multilevel city skyline, something overwhelming that would keep him from thinking of anything else. The neighbors who were barbecuing steaks across the way just weren't very distracting.

Even gazing at the sky didn't help. As a boy he used to lie for hours in the dewy grass behind the house, staring up at the stars, finding the constellations. The lure of the sky had been enough to block out the arguments that were often raging within his family home.

Maybe it was because the sky no longer seemed as vast. Or perhaps it was the lack of damp sun-warmed ground beneath his back. For whatever the reason, tonight's sky couldn't block out anything.

Especially not Cassandra's face as she had looked when he had kissed her so brutally.

He had handled tonight poorly. He would give anything to take back that kiss or those angry, accusing words about her having a lover in New York. He knew that wasn't true, but he had lost his head at the knowledge that she was leaving him.

Remembering his anger, Daniel flexed his hands against his jean-clad thighs. He had actually wanted to hurt her. That frightened him. Not because he thought he could have ever given in to the impulse. But because it reminded him so painfully of his parents.

He could see them now. His pretty blond mother and the fiery black-haired Irishman she had married against her parents' wishes. He would cuss her. She would scream and slap him. And he would hit her right back. They would carry on until the man who had lived next door would come over and separate them, a task Daniel had taken on as soon as he was old enough to put himself in the middle of their battles.

And afterward his father would pack his bags and leave. And his mother would drink. And, as often as not, she would vent on Daniel her rage and frustration with his father.

Daniel knew he would never quite forgive his mother for the way she had treated him. He would never understand why she would want to hurt a child. But tonight he had tasted something close to her often violent anger. He had seen how very easy it would be to lose control. And he was never going to feel that way again.

God, Cassandra, I'm so sorry.

Those were the words he should have spoken, instead of hurling that angry remark at her as he left. He wouldn't blame her if she got on a plane and never looked back. All during their little scene tonight, he had not once told her he loved her. And that was the most important thing he could have said. But no. He had been as selfish as he had accused her of being.

It was just that the thought of losing her again was so hard for him to take. To have her love and lose it twice in one lifetime was too much to expect any man to endure.

But that was still no excuse for his behavior, and he couldn't leave things as they were. If Cassandra was determined to leave—as no doubt she was—then he didn't want her to go without an apology. He had to tell her how ashamed he was.

He should call her. Right now, before he had too much time to think about it.

Daniel had just reached the glass doors that separated the dining room from the patio when the phone rang. Hoping against hope that it would be Cassandra, he sprinted inside.

The caller wasn't Cassandra. It was Matt. The boy's voice dissolved into tears right after he identified himself, and Daniel couldn't make any sense of what he was saying.

"Slow down," Daniel said. "Tell me what's wrong."

"I did it," Matt sobbed. "I'm sorry. I was so mad at her for leaving. I did it."

The blood froze in Daniel's veins. "What did you do, Matt? Tell me."

"The school . . ."

"Yes?"

"It's on fire. I didn't know she was still there."

With those words, Daniel felt his world slow to an agonizing crawl. He dropped the phone. He went to the door. He came back and discovered Matt had hung up. With the horrifying picture Matt's words had painted so imprinted on his mind, it seemed to take hours to dial the fire department and tell them there might be a woman inside that burning old warehouse. He didn't wait to ask if the fire had already been reported.

And he had no idea how he drove to the school.

But till his dying day he would remember the hour-long minutes that passed after he got there. The scene unfolded in flashes.

Wailing sirens.

Lung-choking smoke.

Orange flames licking out of first-floor windows like greedy dragon's tongues.

An inferno no one could survive.

But she had to be alive. Had to be.

"She's on the roof!"

That shout sent him forward until two firemen dragged him back. Someone held him behind the fire trucks, and in the confusion of smoke and water and desperate men, he couldn't even see the roof. All he could do was pray, something he hadn't really done since midway through his childhood, when he had decided even God couldn't make his parents love each other. Or him.

If Cassandra lived, he promised that would be all he needed. Whether or not she really loved him. Whether or not she left him for New York or for a dozen other men. That wouldn't matter. As long as he knew she was alive. Daniel closed his eyes and prayed for that and that alone.

When he looked up again, a fireman was carrying her toward him, shouting that she was fine.

Daniel decided all his other prayers had gone unheeded so that he could have this one. And that was just one more thing to be thankful for.

Ordinarily she loved being pampered. But as she woke up for the second day in a row at the hospital, Cassandra decided enough was enough. A person could take only so much of long-stemmed roses and boxes of candy and plumped-up pillows and a succession of visitors.

All those things were very nice if you were really ill. But she was fine. If there was still smoke in her lungs, she couldn't tell it. Her only other injury was the scratch on her leg, suffered when she had fallen on the roof. She admitted to having had a few black moments then. However, she had known it would be okay. After all, she had used her very own phone on her very own desk to call in the fire and tell them she would be up on the roof. The first floor and the wooden stairs had been engulfed in flames by the time she even knew there was a spark. But she had had enough time to get her purse out of the desk drawer.

She really wasn't traumatized, and she really didn't need to stay in the hospital. What she wanted was to go look at the damage to the school. And to find Daniel. He was the one person who hadn't come by the hospital, and they had a great deal to clear up between them.

That decision made, she got up and dressed and left the hospital before her doctor even made rounds.

As her taxi turned the corner of the street where the school was, Cassandra felt a lump rise in her throat. Her school was now little more than a blackened, burned-out shell.

After the cab was gone, she stood on the cracked sidewalk and mourned for a moment, paying little attention to the early Sunday morning traffic that trickled down the street at her back. Then a car door slammed, and when she looked up she saw Daniel walking toward her. A trace of panic rose inside her and was quickly squashed. There was no reason to be nervous. She just had to tell him exactly how she felt.

He said nothing as he approached her, and for a few minutes he joined her in staring at the ruined building. "If possible, it looks worse than the first time I saw it."

His light tone made her smile, despite her sadness. "But not by much, right?"

He turned his attention to her. "Are you doing okay?"

"I ran away from the hospital."

"I know. They called your parents, and your father called me. I figured you'd be here."

That surprised her. "Why would you know that?"

"Something just told me." Slowly, almost cautiously, he took her hand. "You should have stayed until the doctor released you."

"I had things to do." Cassandra let her fingers lace through his. "Have you seen Matt?" she asked, turning to face him.

Daniel nodded. "He's doing as well as I guess can be expected. He's worried that he hurt you. He didn't intend to. You know that, don't you? The lights were out. He didn't look at the parking lot until he came out. That's when he saw your car and then saw the light come on in your office."

"If I hadn't turned the air conditioner up to maximum level, I might have heard him downstairs."

"Well, whenever you can, he'd probably like to see you. He spent the last two nights in a juvenile detention center. I had Mr. Black call a few people and pull a few strings. Matt'll be going to a well-recommended foster home today. I didn't think he needed to be at home. I want his family investigated before he ever goes back there."

"Good. I think it's pretty obvious there are strange things being said and done by his mother."

"Who knows?" Daniel murmured, looking back at the school. "Maybe all his mother needs is some help."

"I hope so."

Daniel's hand tightened on hers. "I feel responsible for this, you know."

"That's ridiculous."

"No, if I had kept my cool—"

"And if we hadn't argued," she completed for him. "And if Matt hadn't still been here. Daniel, I've been going through all of this in my head ever since it happened. We couldn't have known what he would do."

"But that's not all." He ducked his head, as if looking at her was difficult. Then he met her gaze straight on. "I feel awful about the way I acted. I lost my head, Cassandra. I didn't mean the things I said or did. I stayed away from the hospital because I didn't know if you would want to see me. I didn't want to upset you. Please, will you forgive me?"

"Daniel, I understand," she whispered. "There's nothing to forgive." She put her hand to his cheek, and he pressed a kiss in the palm.

His voice was hoarse. "I thought I had lost you in the fire. I prayed that you wouldn't die."

"I was doing some pretty heavy-duty praying myself." Cassandra felt tears fill her eyes. "I just wanted to see you again. To tell you that I love you, that I've always loved you."

And that'll hold me forever, he thought. Then he pulled her into his arms, murmuring, "I love you, too, Cass. Don't ever forget that."

She cried softly. "Stupid time to be crying, isn't it?" she choked out.

"No," he murmured against her hair. She still smelled of smoke, and that reminded him of how close he had come to losing her. He hugged her even tighter.

She pulled out of his arms, and while wiping the tears from her cheeks, she looked back at the school. "I'm going to have to build another school."

He looked at her in surprise. "On this site?"

She lifted her chin. "I don't know that yet. But I know I have to rebuild. I want something big and solid that you can't laugh at."

He grinned, thinking of the next monstrosity Cassandra might find. "I'll help," he promised. "I'll start scouting around and getting some estimates about rebuilding here while you're in New York—"

"I'm not going to New York."

Something bright and beautiful exploded inside Daniel's chest at the look in her eyes. But he wanted to make one thing very clear. "Much as I want you here, Cass, don't stay for me. You can only stay for yourself."

"There's nowhere else I want to be. I was on my way to tell you that when I smelled smoke the other night."

"It's just one disaster after another with us, isn't it?"

"All's well that ends well." A smile peeked through her lingering tears. "Wanna come and live in a haunted house with me?"

"Only if you buy a rug for that living-room floor. It might get kind of cold this winter."

"Oh, Daniel." Cassandra threw her arms around his neck. "Marry me. Please. Tomorrow. I think our entire lives is a long enough courtship."

"Sure. I'll even marry you today." He lowered his lips toward hers. "We'll do it right after I kiss you."

Breathing a happy sigh, Eugenia stepped back from the fireplace mantel. There, she thought, admiring the newest addition to her collection of framed photographs. Cassandra and Daniel looked just right next to Liz and Nathan.

Behind her there was a disapproving sniff, and Eugenia turned around. Jeannette, the maid who had traveled from France with her, was wheeling a tea cart into the room.

"Tell me this much," Jeannette demanded. "Would it have hurt Cassandra to have a nice big wedding? All we did was go stand out in the garden. She didn't even have a long dress."

"Now, Jeannette. You know our Cassandra. She just couldn't be bothered. She has a new house, and she's trying to find a new place for her school—"

"That's still no good reason, *chérie*."

Smiling at the woman's disgust, Eugenia took a seat on the sofa. "Well, there's always Maggie, Jeannette."

"Maggie. Hah!"

"Well, don't lose heart. At least she had the good sense to dump that clod named Don."

Jeannette shook her graying head. "I say you'll be married before our Maggie makes up her mind about anyone."

"Don't be silly."

With a decided twinkle in her brown eyes, Jeannette fussed over the arrangement of a plate of cookies. "Mr. Herbert Black is not a bad catch."

Eugenia adopted a stern expression. "Thank you, Jeannette, for that observation. I'll call you if I need anything else this afternoon."

"Oui, madame." With a last chuckle, the maid disappeared into the foyer.

Eugenia fussed with the skirt of her dress and glanced at the clock. Herbert was a little late today. How very unlike him. He was such a gentleman. If she were just a bit younger...

Goodness, what was she saying? Age didn't matter when it was really love. Her gaze fell once again on the picture of Cassandra and Daniel. The passage of time didn't matter, either. Look how long it had taken those two to finally get together. Practically their entire lives. She and Herbert could wait a little longer, too, for that matter.

Because first there was Maggie to deal with.

And as Jeannette had said, Maggie was going to be a problem.

"Oh, dear," Eugenia murmured and nodded at the photos on the mantel. "At least I can go to sleep tonight knowing two of my girls are settled at last."

She smiled, gazing at the happy young faces, remembering what it was like to be young and in love.

*　　*　　*　　*　　*

With two of her "treasures" happily married, Aunt Eugenia prepares for her final conquest. But can even the most determined of matchmakers coax Maggie's heart out of hiding? Find out in THE HIDDEN PEARL, an April Silhouette Desire!

SILHOUETTE®
Desire™

COMING NEXT MONTH

#553 HEAT WAVE—Jennifer Greene
Kat Bryant had always been cool to neighbor Mick Larson, but when she was forced to confront him about neglecting his motherless daughters sparks flew and the neighborhood really heated up!

#554 PRIVATE PRACTICE—Leslie Davis Guccione
Another Branigan-O'Connor union? According to Matthew Branigan and Bridget O'Connor—never! But when Bridget caught a glimpse of Matt's bedside manner, her knees got weak and her temperature started rising....

#555 MATCHMAKER, MATCHMAKER—Donna Carlisle
Old-fashioned chauvinist Shane Bartlett needed a wife and it was Cassie's job to find him one—an impossible task! But the search was surprisingly easy. These two opposites were the perfect match.

#556 MONTANA MAN—Jessica Barkley
He thought she was a spoiled socialite. She thought he was a jerk. Could Montana man Brock Jacoby ever tame a frisky filly like Jamaica McKenzie?

#557 THE PASSIONATE ACCOUNTANT—Sally Goldenbaum
Accountant Jane Barnett didn't like things she couldn't control—things like relationships—but Max Harris was proof that an emotional investment could yield a high return in love and happiness!

#558 RULE BREAKER—Barbara Boswell
Women never said no to rebel blue blood Rand Marshall, March's *Man of the Month*—but Jamie Saraceni did. One rejection from her and this rule breaker's bachelor days were numbered.

AVAILABLE NOW:

● SILHOUETTE®
Desire ™

Silhouette Special Edition®

proudly presents

Taming Natasha
by
NORA ROBERTS

In March, award-winning author Nora Roberts weaves her special brand of magic in TAMING NATASHA (SSE #583). Natasha Stanislaski was a pussycat with Spence Kimball's little girl, but to Spence himself she was as ornery as a caged tiger. Would some cautious loving sheath her claws and free her heart from captivity?

TAMING NATASHA, by Nora Roberts, has been selected to receive a special laurel—the Award of Excellence. Look for the distinctive emblem on the cover. It lets you know there's something truly special inside.

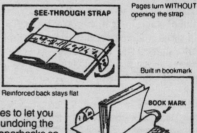

SILHOUETTE DESIRE

Another bride
for a Branigan brother!

"Why did you stop at three Branigan books?"
S. Newcomb from Fishkill, New York, asks.

We didn't! We brought you Jody's story, Desire #523,
BRANIGAN'S TOUCH in October 1989.

"Did Leslie Davis Guccione write any more books
about those Irish Branigan brothers?"
B. Willford from Gladwin, Michigan, wants to know.

And the answer is yes! In March you'll get a chance to
read Matt's story, Desire #553—

PRIVATE PRACTICE
by Leslie Davis Guccione

**You won't want to miss it because
he's the last Branigan brother!**

BRAN-1

At long last, the books you've been waiting for by one of America's top romance authors!

DIANA PALMER
DUETS

Ten years ago Diana Palmer published her very first romances. Powerful and dramatic, these gripping tales of love are everything you have come to expect from Diana Palmer.

In March, some of these titles will be available again in **DIANA PALMER DUETS**—a special three-book collection. Each book will have two wonderful stories plus an introduction by the author. You won't want to miss them!

Book 1
SWEET ENEMY
LOVE ON TRIAL

Book 2
STORM OVER THE LAKE
TO LOVE AND CHERISH

Book 3
IF WINTER COMES
NOW AND FOREVER

Silhouette Books®